Break
By Tarra Blaize

Layla Roads' life is a laundry list of irony. Trailer trash. High school dropout. Beautiful liar. Highly skilled computer hacker. And one additional, extraordinary gift: the ability to see the demons and angels engaged in a ferocious battle on the urban streets at night.

When kidnappers hold her brother, Layla finds herself up to her neck in a plot to bring down a powerful blood demon. A crude, sexual, violent demon who kills without flinching, pushes her buttons, and looks at her with too-knowing eyes. What's worse is she feels an answering tug of desire.

It doesn't take Gethin long to figure out he has a pretty traitor on his hands—and that she's being blackmailed. As a lone human female her quest to save her brother is hopeless— just like the attraction between them. For even if Gethin helps her save all she holds dear, she can never be his...

Warning: Includes a devilish demon, a heroine caught between a rock and a hard place, several magical battles, and the steamy backseat of a car.

Deals with Demons
By Victoria Davies

In a world filled with magic, demons and death, Talia survives using her inborn ability to sense and track demons. A handy skill for a demon hunter. There's one demon, though, who's never far from her mind or her heart.

Years ago Devlin saved Talia from the murderous demon who killed her family. The memory of him has haunted her ever since the night she fled his home, her body branded with a permanent reminder of his lust—and her humiliation.

Now he's back at her door with an offer she can't refuse. He's found the one who killed her family, and he'll help her kill the monster. For a price. One last heated night in her arms.

Temptation and the chance for revenge are too much for Talia to resist. However, once bound to Devlin in an unbreakable deal, Talia realizes too late there's more at stake than the death of her nightmares. Her heart wasn't supposed to be part of the bargain...but she should have known to expect anything when she made a deal with this demon.

Warning: This title contains hot demons and hotter sex. Author advises caution when making deals with the damned.

My Avenging Angel
By Madelyn Ford

It's Victoria Bloom's twenty-fifth birthday. But is she out celebrating? Oh, no. She's in a stuffy old attic with the Three Stooges—a.k.a. her so-called spirit guides. There's a demon who wants her dead, the same one that killed her mother two decades ago. No worries, say the Stooges. All she has to do is summon an angel. What could go wrong?

Well, plenty when you summon the wrong angel. The next thing Tory knows, she's got one very bad-ass, pissed-off and sexy Archangel on her hands.

Michael, mighty warrior, leader of an elite team of demon killers, is shaking in his heavenly combat boots. Not because he finds all humans distasteful. But because he'd rather face Lucifer himself than the woman his soul has just recognized as his mate. Binding himself to a mortal, one who will eventually die, is the one path he's sworn never to follow.

It's too late now; his fate is sealed. With one touch, she becomes as necessary to him as the air he breathes. He will move heaven and earth to protect her—but against a demon as powerful as Asmodeus, heaven and earth may not be enough...

Warning: This book contains one bad-ass Archangel with a fiery, um, sword, a witch who blows things up, one nasty demon who is trying to kill them both, and ghosts who make interfering their mission. Steamy sex is had, even with the voyeur ghosts— though Tory is still blushing.

Angels & Demons

SAMHAIN
PUBLISHING

Samhain Publishing, Ltd.
577 Mulberry Street, Suite 1520
Macon, GA 31201
www.samhainpublishing.com

Angels & Demons
Print ISBN: 978-1-60928-070-3
Break Copyright © 2011 by Tarra Blaize
Deals with Demons Copyright © 2011 by Victoria Davies
My Avenging Angel Copyright © 2011 by Madelyn Ford

Editing by Heidi Moore
Cover by Kanaxa

Break, ISBN 978-1-60928-041-3
First Samhain Publishing, Ltd. electronic publication: May 2010
Deals with Demons, ISBN 978-1-60928-042-0
First Samhain Publishing, Ltd. electronic publication: May 2010
My Avenging Angel, ISBN 978-1-60928-043-7
First Samhain Publishing, Ltd. electronic publication: May 2010
First Samhain Publishing, Ltd. print publication: April 2011

Contents

Break

Tarra Blaize

Dedication

For Kirill, Louise and Danielle. You made me believe this was a matter of when, *not* if.

Chapter One

The sheer sexuality of the blood demon shook Layla Roads down to her core every time her gaze met his heavy-lidded red eyes. Through the transparent walls of her high-tech cubicle, she had a clear view of him prowling across the empty office with all the dangerous, lithe grace of a panther. Given how his eyes fixed upon her with blatant hunger, she couldn't help feeling as if she were the prey. Prey that, as casually as possible, hid the computer document she'd been in the process of memorizing and pulled up another one on-screen.

There was no one in the office besides her and Gethin. The downtown LA cityscape that sprawled out behind her through the floor-to-ceiling glass walls had yet to be tinted with the orange hues of morning. In the teeming metropolis that extended for miles beyond the heart of the urban jungle, most humans remained in bed behind locked doors, pretending to be safe from the shifting shadows of the night. Night was the battleground for the demons who had escaped from Hell and the angels who wished to push them back in.

The snowy white carpet beneath her heels would soon be stained black with blood. She didn't know when, just that it was a matter of time. Her trembling fingers removed the prim plastic glasses from her face to check the wire core visible through the gray frames of her glasses. A bad habit, but one she hadn't been able to break yet. The information she was memorizing was the only thing that could save her brother's life, but it did nothing to save her own. She was well aware that she was a liability. What demons did to liabilities caused her to wake up night after night drenched in her own sweat and muffling screams of terror.

Perhaps the air demons would be merciful and kill her quickly and painlessly once her role in their scheme was done. If they left her behind Gethin would know that she had betrayed him, and she knew very well what he was capable of. His vengeance came from a deeper, uglier part of Hell than theirs did.

She had decided long ago that Gethin never slept. Despite this, there were never signs of exhaustion on his face, just carefully controlled violence and good old-fashioned lust that never failed to ignite a matching heat in her. This morning was no exception. The flimsy door to where she worked swung open with a speed that made her jump in her chair, even though she'd steeled herself.

"Ms. Gills." His voice was darker, deeper than the crevices his kind had crawled from, she thought bitterly. It was underscored with pure steel. Heat too—a weapon he used on her without mercy. He wanted her. He'd made it clear by the second day. Anyway, anywhere. In his bed. On her desk. On his desk. On the floor. Against the wall. And no matter how much indifference or discouragement she threw at him, that list grew longer and longer with every passing day. If she'd been exactly who she pretended to be, then who knew? Perhaps then she could act on the desire he stoked. But she wasn't Ms. Lana Gills as he thought she was. So she could never let it go further than words.

There was no hesitation showing on the hard, angled planes of his face or in his stride. His dark eyebrows formed a heavy, disapproving line across his forehead as he stalked behind her and pulled out the umpteenth hair clip she'd purchased, letting her heavy hair tumble down about her shoulders.

The heat of his fingers burned her scalp as if he'd branded her. "That," she said in the most frosty voice possible, "was uncalled for." Her voice didn't shake the way she worried it would.

Gethin simply sat on the corner of her desk and tilted her face up with a relentless hand. She didn't fight his superior strength, especially as he opened his other fist to let small pieces of silver rain down on her lap. She scowled at him, meeting his intense gaze squarely. "You owe me a new hair clip."

He raised an eyebrow. "I thought I'd told you to keep your hair down, Ms. Gills. It suits you." His gaze, crimson red where hers was brown, moved slowly from her eyes to caress the golden curls he'd just released. She'd been warned he had a thing for blondes. They'd been right.

"I generally find that women with tight buns are restricting their sexuality."

She couldn't help it. She snorted. "This, sir, is a workplace."

He grinned wolfishly, and her heart skipped a beat. Whether it did so because the rare humor that graced his face made him even more desirable or because he was fooling around with her bloodstream again, she didn't know. She'd once made the mistake of accusing him of elevating her heart rate as blood demons were able to do. She'd nearly ended up flat on her back on top of his desk, shirt unbuttoned, skirt around her waist, begging for more.

Well, if she had to be honest, she *had* ended up there, but given how quickly she'd come to her senses and scrambled away, it didn't count.

"This may be a workplace, Ms. Gills, but there's more than office space in this building." He casually reached out with one large hand and stroked her inner thigh right where her pencil skirt ended. Heat rushed towards the spot. Could Gethin somehow sense her blood rushing to the surface of her skin as her nerves went on overload? She had to wear pants. Really. The only problem was, after one week working for Gethin, someone had broken into her company apartment and stolen all of her sensible work clothes. She could still remember her outrage when she opened her closet door one morning and found her clothes stolen and replaced with row upon row of blouses, skirts, and sheer undergarments secretaries would only wear on the silver screen. Judging by the cool smile on his face when she came to work wearing the most modest combination possible, she was fairly certain he was responsible. After all, who else in this office was enough of an ass to do so?

He scraped lightly with his nails down the sheer nylon of her tights. Trying to disguise the jolt of her body, she reached out to pick up her steaming mug of coffee. Her hand shook too much to lift it. Too much caffeine, she told herself, despite the fact that she had yet to take her first sip. She slid her glasses back on and turned her attention to numerous rows of symbols scrolling slowly down her computer screen.

He glanced at her monitor. "Is that the document I asked you to track down in the database?"

She nodded.

"Email it to me. Now. This document isn't your responsibility any longer. Don't change the format."

She knew very well why the format of the symbols had to be preserved. They weren't symbols after all. She'd finally put together all the patterns she'd been agonizing over day and night. The coded words and numbers in the endless data she was able to access as she faxed reports and emailed spreadsheets were cleverly disguised as financial market data and weaponry orders.

Mission accomplished.

She'd cracked the code.

Never before had she been any kind of undercover spy or deep-rooted special agent. She was just Layla, a con artist with the ability to disguise herself and the brilliance to tackle almost anything related to a computer. She also could see paranormal beings when they had shielded themselves from human eyes. Yes, she, trailer-park trash extraordinaire, was one of the few humans who could see what the angels and demons were up to, day after day, week after week, year after year ever since Hell had overflowed five years ago.

A pity she had that rare ability, because she wouldn't have gotten into this mess otherwise. A mess with gorgeous dark curls and red eyes that could go from ice to lava in the space of a second. While she had so far avoided his fury, his passion would be her downfall. Why could he not be as needlessly cruel a demon as the others so he could go firmly into her "evil" category? She knew of other demon assassins, ones who made deranged human serial killers look like Bambi, for crying out loud.

But Gethin seemed...different. As if he had some sort of a purpose, a moral code, and he channeled his violence purely into political assassinations. His calling card was nicking his target with a bullet and bleeding them dry despite any medical attempts to save the victim. But what truly terrified her were the long drawn-out tortures done in the lower levels of the building to get information. Tortures he'd refer to in a calm, detached manner, warning her that he wouldn't be back for five hours. *Hold my calls and reach my cell phone for emergencies only. I'll be in the basement digging for data.*

She'd been shown the basement on the second day. It was a large maze of empty rooms with sinks and drains, chairs and tables. All bloodstained. All so silent that she could still hear the echo of doomed screams ricocheting from wall to wall, forever trapped in this never-ending violence gripping them all.

"Ms. Gills?"

Her attention snapped back. She flushed. "Yes?"

"Is that an answer to my question?"

"What did you say?" She thought back to what he might have asked while she was lost in thought but drew a blank.

"You do sleep naked then." His fangs flashed.

Shoving her glasses firmly back up her nose, Layla swiveled her chair away from him and towards her computer screen, offense written in every rigid line of her body. "I've got work to do, Gethin. If you want it done, you really ought to leave. Now." She glanced back at him, hoping he'd get the hint and leave her in peace.

The blasted blood demon just smiled. "Check your inbox. I need to find a demon and I need him found by yesterday. Start now. Forget locating that human. I'll dump that on someone else."

"I've already located the human, if the data you're referring to was sent at three this morning."

She had the distinct pleasure of seeing genuine surprise flash across his face. "So fast? My goodness, Ms. Gills, you may just be worth the obscene paycheck I give you."

"As if you ever doubted it. Stop bothering me and I'd be even more productive. Then I'd be able to demand a raise."

"So that you could buy more asexual clothing and hair clips?"

Her eyes widened. A freely given admission of guilt was too good to be true. "That was you then? With my clothes?"

His face was inscrutable again. "Do your work, Ms. Gills. I'll be back in here at eleven to make sure you've made headway. Until then, I'll be in the basement."

Her stomach made a long, sickening turn. "I see."

"Do you want to watch?"

"No!" It came out more vehemently than she'd intended it

to.

"No interest in seeing what happens to my enemies? What I do to those people who you locate? How long it takes them to crack, split open and spill out words faster than blood?" He loomed over her chair, gripping the armrests so hard she knew from experience that there would be dents in the metal. His voice was no longer playful or teasing. It was harsh, raw and powerful, and she could almost taste the blood he lusted after.

The carved muscles underneath his shirt expanded as the bloodlust legendary to his kind took hold. Her breath quickened as her blood began to race, and she closed her eyes, struggling to break out of the hypnotic trance he wove around her. This is how she'd ended up on his desk the last time, legs locked around his powerful waist as she dug her nails into the corded strength in his arms. Not again.

"I've no interest in anything except being left alone."

He laughed sharply, relinquishing control of her body so abruptly she felt dizzy.

"You say one thing, but your body says another." He turned and headed towards the door as she did her best to not stare at the way his tailored suit hugged the contours of his behind. "By next month, Ms. Gills, I promise I'll have you naked and willing in my bed. With my fangs deep inside your femoral artery. Research that if you have free time."

She didn't have to. The jolt of desire told her that she was just as sick as he was.

Taking off her glasses, Layla rubbed the bridge of her nose as she sat back, exhausted. She had just finished the latest round of data memorization and needed a break. Just two minutes. But a glance at the clock told her it was nearing eleven, and Gethin was nothing if not punctual. Sure enough, the elevator doors on the other side of the office slid open and he strode out, just as indifferent to the blood on his shirt as the others in the office were. She gave up pretending she was doing something and simply dropped her face in her hands, not looking up even when she heard her door open and shut.

Her glasses fell with a clatter when Gethin dropped a folder stuffed with papers onto her desk.

"These need to be filed."

Layla tried to keep the dismay off her face as she stood with the folder, but judging by the irritation on Gethin's face, she'd failed.

"Filing not good enough for the princess, Ms. Gills?" he taunted softly, taking a small step to bring his body close to hers. She looked up to meet his probing stare, hating how effortlessly dominant he was just by height alone. She could have sworn the heat of his body reached hers, and her blood began to race. She wondered if he was causing it—or if it was just her traitorous hormones.

Filing was beneath her job level, but she'd have no qualms if it didn't interfere with the time she needed to memorize the names and addresses she'd begun to decipher. But what could she do? "Certainly not," she ground out, well aware that she was doing a piss-poor job of acting like it. "Is this the entire pile?"

"Looks like it'll take you two hours. I've got a meeting that should last around three hours. Afterwards I'll have some more names for you to research. Now go." His eyes became distant, as they always did when he spoke about his projects. Layla couldn't help but wonder if after the attack it would be her name he'd be researching, her information he'd be uncovering. She dared not speculate how he'd kill her if he found her. Her body grew cold with sudden terror—he would surely torture her if he ever found out she was a spy, and she would be in the basement with him for more than a few hours. The worse the betrayal, the longer the time—and she'd heard rumors of it lasting weeks, months even, before he'd finish.

"Very well, then." She attempted to disguise her fear as impatience. Turning sharply on her heel, she headed out of her room, gripping the papers so hard that her knuckles turned white.

She was excellent at hiding. Good at masking her true feelings. More than adequate in the detective work he asked her to do. But it had been frightening how quickly he located the people he wanted on those rare times she'd been unable to uncover names and he'd taken on the project himself. It was terrifying to see their names in the papers afterwards, headlines announcing yet another mysterious—and at times downright gruesome—assassination.

She tried not to think about the vital role she played in their deaths. Her brother's life was at stake, and given that Gethin's assassinations more often than not tended to be big, bad demons and corrupted humans, she could even say they deserved it. But sometimes...sometimes it wasn't enough. Even though she knew it would have happened without her, all too often she felt as though she'd pulled the trigger herself.

But the names she'd uncovered from the decoded files— there was no way she could possibly memorize them all. How many had the air demons been expecting? Twenty? Fifty? There were hundreds upon hundreds, with more coming each day. Names of people, companies, nicknames, locations. She was expected to memorize them all. She'd need days, and the air demons had given her five weeks, tops. She'd already used up over four of them.

If his meeting would last three hours she needed to finish the filing in record time so she could memorize, memorize, memorize before he got back.

One hour and ten minutes later Layla strode out of the bathroom, paper towels clutched tightly around her index finger. She'd never filed so quickly, and though the cost was a wicked cut from a metal tab, it was well worth it. She had almost two hours to knock out her goal of fifty names and addresses before she had to deal with another assassination project for Gethin.

"Lana!" Todd was at her desk looking worried. Accustomed to being called Ms. Gills by all others, it took Layla a moment to respond. Todd was one of the few bright spots in her life right now. A quiet, friendly blood demon, nowhere near as powerful as Gethin, he was always there when she needed help. She'd grown closer to him than she'd anticipated and had to struggle daily to keep a friendly distance.

"Lana, I'm so sorry, but—what happened to your hand?"

His gaze was level with her face and he even made an attempt to hide his growing fangs, bless him. If it had been any demon other than Todd, she'd worry that his bloodlust would result in her being an unintentional lunch. But Todd had the kindest heart she'd ever known. Too bad he assisted a murderer and drank blood in an office where she was an undercover spy. Otherwise, he might have been the perfect guy to ask out on a date.

The blood had soaked completely through the paper towel. "Oh, drat. Nothing major, Todd. Just a paper cut of epic proportions. I've got some first aid at my—" Her voice trailed off and the blood rushed from her face as she registered what Todd was holding in his cupped hands.

Her glasses.

Snapped in two.

Layla cried out. Her stomach clenched in horror and her lungs struggled to take in air. Terror made her head feel light, and she lurched forward to grab her glasses, heedless of her injured finger. Sure enough, the transmitting device inside the frames had snapped cleanly in half. Todd's mistake had sent her blackmailers the emergency signal. The air demons were about to attack, and she had barely any data ready.

Chapter Two

Todd grabbed her arms and carefully lowered her into her chair, kneeling before her. "Lana, I'm so sorry. They were on your desk and I didn't see them and I put something on top of them."

Lips numb, she asked, "When did this happen?"

Todd's face filled with guilt. "About fifteen minutes after the boss sent you off filing. It's all my fault. You're in shock. I'll get them replaced. I promise."

She didn't answer. She had to download the files onto a PDA, no matter the risk of someone detecting it. When the small receiver in the wire core of her spectacles was broken, it had signaled to her blackmailers that something had gone wrong and that she needed to be removed. She had to have something to show the demons or her brother was gone. Dead. Just like she would be very, very soon.

With a deep breath, she tried to clamp control over a world that had just imploded. "It's not your fault, Todd. It was my fault." The honest words felt bitter in her mouth. "I shouldn't have forgotten them on my desk. I know it can become a nuthouse around here." She turned away, her mind beginning to spit out warnings. She had around five minutes. Five minutes before a portal would open in thin air and the air demons would flood the room, killing all in their efforts to recover the data stored in her brain.

Her brother. Herself. Gethin. Todd. Someone was going to die today, and she'd lost her bargaining chip.

She needed those files. Now. But Todd was still in front of her, his reddish-brown eyes filled with remorse. She needed to save him, somehow. At least him. How to get him to leave?

"Todd, I'm fine. Really. They're just glasses. But, if you don't mind, can you take them over to the optometrist's to get them fixed right now? I'm sorry to be such a bother, but I get headaches when I don't wear them, and I know you've got a lunch break right now."

Todd stood, visibly relieved. "Of course. Want to come with and grab lunch? The boss is still in his meeting, and we could get back here in an hour or so if we leave now."

She forced herself to smile at him. "I'd love to, but actually, the reason I rushed through filing is because I remembered an assignment he gave me yesterday that I totally forgot about. I just want to download some stuff onto my PDA so I can have a chance to read them whenever possible. I've got other small errands I need to do, and reading on the way will help save my rear end."

Todd's eyes crinkled slightly as he gave his trademark sweet smile. "Let's avoid getting you into trouble, shall we? If you fall behind, I'd be glad to run some errands for you. Lana—" he paused, delicately cleared his throat, "—you're dripping blood everywhere. Do you need help?"

"Thanks, Todd, but I've got it." She didn't need a demon going crazy on her right now. She grabbed a tissue and started to mop at the cut she'd forgotten all about. Her finger stung anew with a vengeance. "The glasses are already a huge favor."

"No problem," he assured her and hurried off, cradling the frames as delicately as he could. She instantly turned towards her laptop, grabbed her PDA and set up the downloads required.

Four minutes, approximately.

She grabbed a piece of paper and began to jot down some of the biggest names. If her PDA failed she'd have a hard copy backup. James Elron. New York. Elron Corporation, Vice President. Demon. Marked for assassination. Blood dripped all over the paper, but she didn't care. Tabitha Stevenson. Roy Jacobs. Agatha DeMarcus.

Two minutes later, an observation brought with it a rush of nausea so intense she made a blind grab for her wastebasket.

Gethin's meeting had apparently ended early, and he was striding along the offices, ducking into each one to check up on his employees.

He would reach her in less than a minute, and even a blood demon without his astute observations would see red flags instantly with her heart racing, breath short and blouse dotted with blood. She wrote faster, racing the downloading files. Perhaps if she had thirty very important names the air demons would believe she had gotten as many as she could. She'd scribbled twenty-seven down so far. Twenty-nine. Thirty-three. Spinning her chair so she faced away from the rest of the floor, she folded up the piece of paper and slipped it under her bra. She turned back to end the file download—she'd gotten about a tenth of them—and was reaching for her first aid in the top drawer of her desk when her office door swung open.

"Fucking hell, what did you *do*?"

The unfamiliar cadence to his tone shocked her so much she dropped the first aid cream. "N-nothing," she stammered.

Gethin looked absolutely furious as he strode around the desk, but his voice—there was a thread to it she'd never heard before. One that made her heart lodge in her throat and tears prick her eyes.

"Your heart is racing. You're covered in blood. You're about to hyperventilate."

She held up her finger, morbidly fascinated by the small ribbon of scarlet twisting down her finger to race across her palm. "I think I sliced my finger on a file. I didn't get blood in them. But the carpet here needs to be cleaned before it sets in."

"I don't care about the fucking file or the damn carpet." His fingers wrapped around her upheld wrist as he knelt before her to better examine the injury. Clearly, her sex drive was kicking in overtime before she died, she thought, sardonically amused. Gethin kneeling between her legs almost made her last hours on Earth worth living.

"I've got a Band-Aid..." Her sex drive nearly turned inside out with dark delight when Gethin's mouth closed around her finger. Instinctively, she tried to pull her arm back, but it was like trying to escape a steel trap. She was utterly helpless as Gethin ran his tongue across the cut, his newly elongated fangs whispering across her flesh before he lifted his head. His eyes blazed as he dragged that same tongue around his lips to remove all bloodstains. Her breath hitched in her throat.

"Do you have any idea how good you taste?" he rasped. As if unable to help himself, he lapped one last time at the cut, his rough tongue creating a painful pleasure that fanned across her skin.

She closed her eyes. Shuddered. No, but if it were half as good as she imagined *he'd* taste... "Please let go of me. I've stopped bleeding." Demon saliva had healing properties, but she'd prefer a Band-Aid to playing with fire. "I—I think you've nearly closed the cut back up." The slash had been at least a good inch long. Where it had been weeping blood before, it was nothing but an angry red line now.

He didn't move from his position. He tilted her hand down, his grip heated around her wrist. Entranced, she watched as his other hand lazily traced the contours of her palm. She knew he was watching her face, but she couldn't summon the courage to meet his eyes.

"You certainly bleed a lot, Ms. Gills," he finally said. "Do you often injure yourself filing?"

"No," she whispered. "I'm fine now, thank you." How much time left? A minute? Maybe more? Maybe less? She was on borrowed time. She had no idea when exactly her glasses had been broken, but she could feel the snakes writhing deep inside, every sense, every inch of her skin hyper-alert to what was going on. Muted noises of other workers outside her office. His hot skin pressed demandingly against hers, her hand delicate in comparison to the hard, wide palms of his. The slight scent of coppery blood. She couldn't bring herself to give a damn right now that she was breaking just about every rule in her book. If she was going to die she might as well remember something to put a smirk on her face before her time was done.

"Lana," he whispered roughly. His hands left hers to wrap around the nape of her neck and draw her inexorably forward. He cradled her jaw as he leaned forward to meet her halfway, eyes melting into a hot, flaming crimson, face taut, and his firm lips slanting over hers with no hesitation whatsoever.

She'd barely registered the heat of his mouth when a horrifying noise rent the air, as if Heaven itself were being torn in half. Gethin's lips tore away from hers as he shoved her so hard her wheeled chair slammed into the far wall of her office. Dazed, she realized a slash of blue light had ripped, in midair, right next to where she'd been sitting.

"Air demons!" Gethin roared, and the office exploded.

She scrambled to her feet just as Gethin grabbed her around the waist and flung himself through the glass walls of her cubicle, shattering them as other blood demon warriors rushed towards them. She writhed and twisted, desperately trying to free herself as the air demons poured through the enlarging holes torn in her office, their normally pale blue eyes darkening with their burgeoning powers. More and more portals slashed into existence, and already she saw bodies falling to the floor, throats torn open and wounds gaping.

He continued running, arms locked around her so tightly

her breathing was restricted. She was forced to fall limp in his embrace as he raced full tilt through a maze of hallways, doors and stairs, many of which were only vaguely familiar to her. Having abandoned her attempts to free herself, she concentrated on memorizing the path he took, one hand on her chest to anchor the priceless list of names lest it fall out into the chaos.

Her world flipped again when Gethin halted abruptly, opened a door and flung her into a small room—one that looked strongly barricaded, she realized. She staggered and would have fallen had his hands not gripped her upper arms with bruising force. There were others in here, all looking as terrified as she felt. "My private office is the most guarded from these attacks," he snarled. "Stay here with the other humans. Do not leave. If you leave, you will die. My demons are capable of fending them off, but you don't stand a chance out there. Do you understand?" He shook her, hard, sharpened teeth bared in a snarl, muscles straining against his white shirt.

"You saved me," she whispered, aware that tears were streaking down her face.

He'd been turning away, heading back to the battle that raged on behind them, but he turned at her words and grinned fiercely. The red of his eyes were swirling with dark streaks, and his powerful energy nearly crackled in the air around him. "But of course, Ms. Gills," he drawled. "You owe me a hell of a lot more than a kiss for this, and I fully intend to collect as soon as possible. Lock the door behind me." And he turned and vanished into the labyrinth of the office building.

Heedless of the cries and warnings of the other humans behind her, she waited a few agonizing seconds before she slipped back out. One woman whom she vaguely recognized from the front desk leaped forward to try to pull her back into the safety of the room. She tore herself from the woman's grasp, kicked off her heels and darted the way Gethin had taken her as quietly as possible.

He'd saved her, and the least she could do was get to the air demons before they killed him. She had enough blood on her hands already, and she didn't know if she could live with herself if Gethin was murdered too.

It was in an eerie silence that she tripped over the first body as she rounded a corner at full speed. Pain exploded in her ankle as it twisted, sending her to her knees with a force that promised bruises. Disoriented and dazed, she looked for the obstacle and gagged, the bile rising in her throat sharp and acidic.

She couldn't even tell who or what type of demon it was—its face looked like it had been methodically tortured with a cheese grater. Blood trickled down the mass of pulpy, torn flesh to pool on the floor where her foot had slipped. She jerked away, scrambling on her hands and one knee towards the other side of the hallway. The blood followed, soaking into her skin and smearing a trail of red after her.

She fought her rebelling stomach, but failed. Hunched over, she vomited violently, head spinning so fast she would have fallen had she not been on the ground. *Not my fault, not my fault*, she chanted, but it did nothing to ease her pounding head. So instead, she focused in on her brother's face, with his baby cheeks and the mischievous brown eyes they shared. How grown-up Nathanial had looked in his navy blue uniform as he went into the third grade this year, chin up and never looking behind him as he strode confidently into his new school.

He wasn't on the floor behind her. He wasn't dead. And she had to keep going if she wanted to keep him that way.

With both arms braced on the wall for balance, she struggled upright and limped down the hallway, not even sure where she was going, fighting the waves of pain as each move jarred her ankle. Twisted, she hoped. Not broken. Either way, she was even weaker than before. A sitting duck, really. *But if I get lost now it'll be easy to trace a path back. Just follow the blood.* Just follow all the blood and it always came back to her. The silence pressed in around her, mocking her labored breath and the frantic, uneven pitter-patter of her feet against the cold, white floor.

She felt like she'd been hobbling for hours using the walls for support—though in reality it couldn't have been more than a few minutes—before she heard shouts and screams piercing the air. She must be approaching the main office. Layla touched her chest nervously. The paper with the names was still there. She needed to see an air demon, and she needed to let herself be taken before anyone tracked her down.

And then what, once she was dead? She'd beg the demons to kill her quickly, and dump her body somewhere in this labyrinth of halls, she realized dully. Because if not, Gethin would figure out what happened and go after Nathanial. And all she'd sacrificed would be for naught.

Flattening herself against the wall, she stealthily wiggled her way forward, holding her breath as she peered around the last corner. The air exploded out of her lungs in a gasp of shock, and when she tried to draw it back in it was as if the air had thinned. She'd seen battles rage between demons and angels, but never between two groups of demons.

As opposed to the dark against light superpowers she'd always associated with the war, the room billowed with acrid smoke and violent colors. Blood demons on the far side of the room were throwing up swirling shields in their trademark crimson, using their powers to disrupt the blood flow of their enemies so that either their bodies starved without oxygen or they bled out in just a few short minutes. The air demons were closer to her, manipulating the oxygen in the air, slashing through the shields with dark blue light, ripping rents in the air. As she watched horrified, an air portal tore through the space a blood demon was occupying and tore his body in half.

If she hadn't emptied her stomach before, she would have now. Before she could choose what course of action to take, she heard a now familiar screech behind her. Spinning around and going to the precious piece of paper, she watched as Vyn's head appeared in a small portal in midair about ten feet away from her. She couldn't get closer to him without the blood demons seeing her.

"Human!" Vyn snarled. "Where are the names?"

"I have them," she whispered, trembling from head to toe. "Th-they're right here. Thirty-three names. Thirty-three names and addresses." She hesitantly drew out the piece of paper, shaking her head when he reached out impatiently, beckoning for her to come closer. "Swear. Swear you'll forever and ever leave my brother alone, and never harm him or anyone near him either directly or indirectly. Promise me."

Vyn smiled, a sickly, smarmy smile. "But of course, Layla. And we shall spare you too."

She swallowed hard. "No, you won't."

The smile grew. "You're right. We won't. Come. Now."

"You have to kill me quickly." Tears rose, blurring the battle that rained sparks and poured blood behind Vyn. "You have to leave my body here so that Gethin doesn't realize it was me and go after Nathanial. You have to. Or you'd be indirectly responsible for anything Gethin does to him."

Vyn laughed. "I don't have to do anything, human."

"Swear!" Her voice rose hysterically as she dangled the paper just out of reach. "Swear on your liege lord!"

Vyn's breath hissed out as his face contorted into a snarl, his pale blue eyes narrowing with shock. Very few people knew that the only thing that could bind a demon was his oath to his liege lord. Not every demon had one, but if he did, outright falsehoods were impossible.

"Yes. Swear." She shoved the paper back into her bra, watched his eyes follow the motion greedily. "Swear it, you bastard, or I'll—"

Whatever she was about to say choked in mid-sentence as the portal lengthened and broadened as it grew to accommodate the air demon storming through. She backed up so fast she nearly tripped, but Vyn's hand lashed out and struck her across the face. Her head met the wall and sparks the same color as the air portal danced and swam sickly. She fell to the floor hard, ankle screaming, as Vyn bent over her. Feebly, she kicked and shoved, baring her teeth to sink them into his restraining arm. But he was too strong. He batted her away as if her fists were no more than flies and roughly yanked the piece of paper out of her clothing. Mission accomplished, he struck her once more, and as she lay there stunned, he turned to head back into the portal.

"No!" she cried as she struggled to her knees. "No! No!"

He ignored her, the life of her brother securely in his fist as he prepared to leave.

"How dumb do you think I am?" she screamed. "Those aren't the real names!"

He froze at her bluff and turned around. His cold eyes were nearly pulsating. "Then where are they?"

"In my head." She could make up names, recall names she'd looked up for Gethin, anything. She could do anything, everything. She had to. "I've memorized them. I don't trust you, Vyn. And with damn good reason."

With a frustrated sound, the portal around Vyn began to widen. Layla got to her feet and was heading towards it when Vyn gasped sharply and the portal stopped growing. His gaze went past her shoulder.

"He's blocking the portal," he breathed. "Get here, fast. Give me those names or I assure you, Nathanial will die long after you do."

Layla looked over her shoulder to where Vyn's gaze was riveted in horror. Her shocked stare collided with Gethin's astonished one as he froze in mid-stride. A rent in the air went right by his ear, but he didn't even flinch.

"Layla!" Vyn bellowed, and she looked at him blankly. "You need to crawl through this." Sweat beaded his brow as he struggled against the unseen force that prevented him from getting to her.

Nathanial. She had to save Nathanial.

She started to crawl towards the air demon, not even trying to get to her feet, as a roar that nearly shook the ceiling down drowned out every other sound in battle. Terror filled her mouth with hot sand, and she looked behind her to see Gethin charging towards her. His eyes—God save her—the entire orbs were a vicious blood red, focused on her, murderous rage radiating from every pore. An air demon tried to block Gethin's way—he simply collapsed, blood dotting out of his pores and pouring in rivulets from his nose.

"Layla!" Vyn called out, desperate, reaching out for her, but it was too late. She felt all of Gethin's powers crash over her. Her blood raced, raced so hard that her heart stuttered. Blinding pain flashed through her head and set her limbs on fire. She felt her arms give way, the distant slap as her cheek hit the ground beneath her.

She had to get to Vyn. She had to get to Vyn, or Nathanial would die. But as her vision faded and someone flipped her body over roughly, the last thing she saw was a closing portal transition into a snarling face with hard, red marbles for eyes, eyes in which she saw her own death before darkness mercifully swept her under.

Chapter Three

The pain in Layla's head was the first signal that something was wrong. The sharp stabs at the base of her skull were unrelenting in their rhythm. She shifted in an attempt to avoid whatever was causing it. Instead, she made it worse.

Her mouth felt dry, her skin clammy. Was she sick? No. She would have been in bed, at her apartment. Upon opening her eyes, she realized that being home with the flu would have been, by far, the better scenario.

She was in a tiny room so blindingly pure and devoid of color that she closed her eyes as soon as she opened them. Her body was lying on something hard, lumpy and uncomfortable.

Gethin. The air demons.

Nathanial.

She forced herself to open her eyes and get up, panic fueling the adrenaline rush that coursed unfettered through her body. Aches and bruises screamed in protest, but she ignored them, sitting up straight and forcing her tired eyes to take in her surroundings, analyze what the hell had happened.

Speaking of hell—had she died? Apparently not. She was in a room with white walls, white ceiling and a white floor. She was lying on a small bed, there was what looked like the most primitive of toilets in the corner, and the only exit was a large white door marked only by hairline cracks.

She got up, wincing when she tried to put weight on her

ankle and failed. Hopping to the door revealed what she already suspected—the door certainly could open, but not from her side. This was a cell in all sense of the word—and come to think of it, she didn't even know if it could open. Perhaps Gethin had buried her alive in this small tomb. Or perhaps he was just going to hold her here until she went insane.

He wouldn't have to wait long at all for that to happen, she thought grimly. Because he'd stuck her in here, utterly helpless with Nathanial in dire danger. And there was nothing she could do about it. Nothing at all.

She let her back hit the wall, and then, with a muffled scream, she slammed into the wall. Her whole back stung, but it didn't help. It didn't change anything except prove how thick the walls were—she didn't even hear a muffled thud when she hit it.

But chances were someone was either watching her or guarding her. Keeping quiet might keep her alive longer, but she had to get out, had to get to Nathanial somehow. In the meantime the air demons would probably soon realize the document they'd taken from her was indeed the real deal—hopefully that would keep them absorbed for a few days, long enough for her to get out of there.

"Hello?" she called tentatively.

Nothing.

She knocked firmly on the door. Then she pounded it with her fists until tears poured unchecked and her breath exploded out of her lungs in huge, violent gasps. After what felt like hours, she let her hands remain pressed against the cool surface and placed her forehead between them. "You have to let me out," she whispered. "You don't understand. You have to let me go."

The words were spoken to herself, but to her surprise, she heard a distinct *click-slide-whump* of several locks being opened. The door swung open so fast she didn't have enough time to catch her balance on her injured ankle.

She fell flat on her face, stunned.

"Get up," a familiar voice said harshly.

Startled, she scrambled clumsily to her feet, reaching out a hand without thinking. "Todd! You're alive!" She could have wept in relief. She'd managed to save one person, at least. But any possible happiness was dashed as he shifted to avoid her touch, his sweet face set in angry, unforgiving lines.

"Don't touch me, traitor," he snarled. "Don't even talk, because whatever you'll say will be nothing but a falsehood. And I assure you it is in your best interest to be very honest in the next few hours, because the boss isn't going to let himself be fooled a second time."

Stunned, she let him bind her hands behind her. She couldn't escape. She could try. She still would. But Todd had a hand clamped over her restrained arms and was roughly hauling her down the hallway, turning into another... She felt what little calm she had left in her drain away when she recognized some of the rooms.

She was in the basement.

Without any conscious decision, she jerked her body hard in the opposite direction. His hand slipped with a surprised grunt, and Layla tore off, trying to lean as much weight as she could on her other leg. Her ankle threatened to buckle with each step. Knowing what she would face gave her the strength to keep going until Todd caught up.

"No!" she screamed. "You've got to let me go! You don't understand! I-I—" She choked on the words as Todd simply tossed her over his shoulder and carried her kicking and screaming until he opened a door and dumped her on the ground beyond it. She got one look at his set jaw before he locked her in yet again.

Wishing she could wipe her nose, Layla wearily sat and scooted around until she had her back to the wall She didn't even feel anything but vaguely nauseous when she realized she'd seen this bloodstained table before—on one of her unofficial building tours in her first week.

This was Gethin's playroom, and she was soon to be just another broken toy.

Indeed, she felt like a broken toy as she sat there and wondered miserably how much she could tell Gethin without risking him going after her brother as well.

Her thoughts were interrupted when the door right next to her opened slowly. She didn't need to look at his face to know who was walking in—the weight of authority lay heavily in the air about him.

She didn't know what she expected him to do. Cause her blood to leak from her ears. Pick her up and break her bones. Unleash his bloodlust and drain her.

He certainly seemed to be in the right mood. His entire body was clothed in soft black material. His body seemed tense, coiled and braced for action. He simply stood there, the leathery material of his boots a mere whisper from her bloodstained feet and smudged, grubby legs exposed by huge tears in her pantyhose.

Her skirt was ripped too, high enough that she would have normally turned bright red in embarrassment. But all she felt was a dull pain in her chest. Nathanial.

Neither of them spoke. The silence stretched and spun out endlessly. All the unspoken emotions clouded the air between them as she sensed his stare boring into the top of her bent head as she studiously examined the neat stitches in his black jeans.

And then, as if someone had flipped a switch, he snapped. An unearthly roar ripped from his chest, and the heavy metal table flew into the wall with a mighty heave. The ceiling shook, the ground trembled and a dent the depth of her head appeared where the furniture had landed. The two chairs were next,

35

hurled over and over again as he took out all his rage and frustration on the inanimate objects in the room. She curled up into a little ball and waited.

He finished abruptly, his heavy breaths amplified in the deadened air. On the periphery of her vision, she watched those boots stalk closer, closer, until he was next to her. She didn't have the courage to look up, to see if his hands were reaching for her next, his eyes glowing with a lust soon to be sated with her very own life.

Should she tell him she was blackmailed? If she did he'd ask her what leverage the air demons had over her. She couldn't know for sure if he would save Nathaniel or kill him—and just because she thought Gethin might be a demon she could trust didn't mean she was ready to stake her brother's life on it.

She'd been betrayed enough to know that those closest always stabbed the deepest. A husband? He'd see right through that. Money? That was begging to be murdered where she sat. A threat to her own life? But then there was that gaping hole of why she hadn't just begged him for protection—especially as she had the nagging suspicion that he would have kept her safe, and not only out of sexual attraction.

As she struggled to come up with a believable story, she looked up at him. And flinched.

If she had ever wondered if demons could have anguished souls, her answer would have been found in his eyes.

"I had to," she whispered as he dropped in a fluid harmony of muscle to kneel at her side, one hand stroking her neck almost lovingly.

"I know you're going to kill me. And I accept that. But you have to believe me. I had to do this."

He was silent for a moment. "I don't have to believe a single damn word that comes out of your pretty little lips," he finally whispered huskily. He made no movement to wipe away the sheen of perspiration that coated his bare arms and face, or to brush at the trickle of sweat that slowly traced the hard line of his jaw before dropping down his neck. His eyes were sharp as knives and only inches from her face as he leaned forward. "And what makes you so sure I'm not going to keep you alive?"

She briefly shut her eyes, unable to face his probing assessment. His breath fanned over her averted face, stirring tendrils of her hair. "You have to believe me."

"Why?"

"Because I'm telling you the truth. How can I prove it to you?"

"You can't, of course," he chided her gently. "Many traitors start off by telling me that they're innocent. I must admit, you did a good job. With your nervous attitude, pretty blonde hair, understated appearance... You must have laughed so, having me wrapped around your delicate little finger." His fingers surrounded one of hers and tightened around the joint, demonstrating just how delicate it really was. "And when I start snapping these, you'll scream out how it wasn't your fault. And when you start bleeding, you'll be too busy screaming to lie anymore. And after half your body's mangled beyond recognition—be that in the next hour or the next week—then I'll start taking what you have to say seriously."

"Fine." She was broken. Dull and broken and so tired of it all.

"Fine?"

She didn't have to look at him to see his sardonic expression.

"You're accepting of this being your fate?"

She laughed, her throat dry and hoarse. "I don't really have a choice, do I? But you need to promise me something."

Gethin stiffened, and she grabbed his leg. It was unyielding iron beneath her pleading fingers. "You have to promise me to protect someone. From the air demons. That's all I ask." She expected a refusal, a denial, for him to laugh in her face. Any reaction so that she could launch into a sob story about a false child, to gauge whether he could truly help her.

But instead, he got up, jerked his leg from her grasp and left the room, leaving her shaken and bewildered.

Chapter Four

After being escorted back from a bathroom by a granite-faced Todd, Layla found food waiting for her. Clearly, Todd didn't think she deserved the respite, and slammed the door on his way out. Not knowing when the next meal would come, she ate, and she ate fast. When she had finished the last of the toasted garlic bread layered with cheese, salami and prosciutto—surely Gethin wouldn't kill her while that was still in her stomach—Todd appeared again to silently remove the empty plates and lock the door behind him. She was alone again with nothing to keep her occupied.

She'd gotten bored of limping about, was tired from the random bouts of weeping, and had just finished mentally prepping herself for many more hours of misery when the door opened and Gethin strode in, his face just as blank as Todd's. Damn them both. But what small part of her rejoiced at any kind of company soon faltered and dropped dead at the...*thing* Gethin so casually dragged behind him into the room.

"Is he still alive?" She leaned away nervously as Gethin reached the table where she sat.

Gethin raked the bloody air demon with a contemptuous look as the roped muscles of his arms grew taut with the effort of hauling the dead weight to dump on the table like some sort of grotesque feast. "I damn well hope so. He was screaming just a few minutes ago, and I'd be really fucking pissed if the bastard managed to drop dead before I finished with him."

"You're going to kill him *here*?" Layla gasped. She didn't recognize him beyond being an air demon, but a living thing was a living thing. She scooted her chair away as fast as possible.

"Well, that depends on you, Ms. Gills." He grinned, almost rakishly. The charm didn't spread to his eyes. "I've gotten quite a bit of information from him, and while I'm pretty sure he doesn't mean anything to you, I bet you're just...virginal enough in this whole demon business that you'd let me see if your story syncs up enough to his to give him a peaceful end."

She slumped in her chair, defeated. "Very well. What do you want to know?"

"What happened then, Layla?" Each time he said her real name he let it roll around his tongue as if it were some kind of foreign delicacy, a sort of morsel he wasn't quite sure if he liked yet. The injured air demon was breathing shallowly, but steadily. She kept her eyes focused on a dent in the wall just over Gethin's left ear.

"I—they told me what to expect from you, what I needed to look for and what data I needed to decode. The air demons told me you're trying to find someone important. I don't know who, or why. They want to find this person first, and Vyn's been trying to catch up to whatever information flow you get, but I didn't give him too many names—"

Gethin was silent for a long minute before transitioning to the previous subject. "I want a list of each name you were able to pass on. What were you taught to expect from me?" From his slouched pose to his crossed legs, Gethin might have looked almost careless to the stupidest of observers. Layla wasn't sure what answer he was looking for, so she caught her breath before telling the truth.

"Vyn told me—Vyn being the one in charge of me—he told

me that you liked blondes." She saw his eyebrow rise and hurried on. "He said that you were very violent, and very—um, potent."

Gethin chuckled, leaning forward with his elbows propped on his knees as if watching a particularly intriguing television show. "He actually said I was potent?"

Vyn had told her bluntly that when Gethin wanted to fuck her she'd better go willingly to his bed, but she didn't dare relate that to him. "Something along those lines. I don't quite recall."

"Don't start lying now, Layla," Gethin drawled. His crimson eyes were sensuous and mocking. "I'm pretty sure you remember everything you were told word for word, but if you're too shy to admit you were ordered to play the naughty secretary, then that's fine with me."

Anger made quick work of embarrassment, and Layla straightened in her seat with a glare scorching enough to wither a lesser man. "I assure you, Gethin, that there is nothing I want more than this whole ordeal to end. So please, can we conclude this as soon as possible?"

His face became unreadable, blank where there had been a gleam of laughter before. "I believe I've told you this can only end in one way." Quiet reproof stroked across each of the heartless words he uttered.

"And I believe I told you I've accepted that."

"And you believe me." It was more of a statement than a question.

She nodded, unable to speak. Her hands were wrapped around each other in a death grip.

"Are you so eager to die then?" he asked, softly, so gently that she felt the unmistakable pressure of tears push against the backs of her eyes and coat the back of her throat. "Do you truly have no one to live for?"

Tarra Blaize

I have no one to live for, but someone to die for. She didn't say the words out loud though, and instead fixed her gaze on the injured air demon. He'd stopped bleeding, courtesy of Gethin's power, but he hadn't moved once the entire time. "I'm sure you did a thorough background search on me," she said instead. "Surely you know I've no one."

He made a *tsk*ing sound in the back of his throat. "No family, of course. Quite the childhood you must have had with the rap sheet your parents built between the two of them. Judging by how your father traveled, I assume you stayed at home with your mother?"

Her childhood—or lack thereof—wasn't something she wanted to go into, but she didn't have much of a choice. "My father left when I was very young, yes. I stayed with my mother until I moved out for college."

"Which you didn't even graduate from. Why did you drop out after your mother died?"

She finally looked at him, expecting to see what she usually saw on other people's faces who knew about her background— pity, scorn, disgust, a shifting of perspective that she was somehow dumber, less capable because she didn't have a pretty piece of paper signed and stamped hanging on her wall. She'd shown all of them.

But instead, she saw something that might have just been understanding.

"I couldn't afford not to work with all with the debt I inherited," Layla said flatly. "And by then I was a legal adult and realized I was good enough at what I did that the people who would pay the most wouldn't care that I hadn't graduated."

"A pretty little hacker then, who's got her balls in some nasty air demon's hands," Gethin mused, almost to himself. "And since it's not family, and not friends given your all-too-obvious loner status, then who are the air demons threatening to kill if you don't finish the mission? Who do you care about so much that you can't even bring yourself to tell me?"

Her mouth felt bone-dry. "I've told you everything I can. They didn't let me know much about their plans. I really don't know anything." Agitated, she bit her lip, realizing with a sinking feeling that very soon she'd have to make an ultimate decision about Nathanial.

"Can't, shan't, won't." Gethin almost hummed the words, stretching his body out luxuriously as if waking up from a particularly delightful nap before he got to his feet. "Well then, I see we've reached the end of what you're willing to say. But do tell me this—when your little friends here were training you for being under my employment, how did they convince you to memorize and prepare all that you needed to know? How did they threaten you about whomever you're still protecting? I've never known them to be particularly eloquent—with words, that is."

He knew. He had to know. But he stood there, his hands shoved in his pockets, the air demon only a foot away, with a calm, almost friendly look on those beautiful features of his.

"They threatened someone I care for," she said slowly, stating only what she was certain he knew.

"Anything else?"

"No." The lie was cold as ash on her tongue.

He reached out and brutally hit the air demon across the face. Layla cringed at the unexpected violence, wrapping her arms around her middle for support as the air demon came to, moaning. When he tried to sit up, he saw Gethin standing over him and collapsed back again with a whimper of terror.

"Hello," Gethin said gently. "I want you to answer me again—was the blonde human tortured when she refused to cooperate or didn't do what was demanded of her in the exact way she was supposed to? Was she ever hurt just for fun, to teach her who was in charge?"

No, don't! Layla wanted to shout out, but the air demon

43

only darted a frightened look her way before answering shakily. "Y-yes, she was hurt whenever she didn't do something the way she was supposed to. But the demons in charge of her made sure there were no marks, sir, because the marks would have t-tipped you off."

"Thank you," Gethin murmured. Something on his face gave Layla all the warning she needed to close her eyes and put her hands over her ears, but there was no mistaking the sickening crack of a neck being snapped. Then strong arms swept her out of her seat so suddenly that all she could do was grab at his wide shoulders as he strode out the door. "We're done here, Layla. No more death today. I promise. We don't need any more pain today. I'm taking you home for the night."

And for some reason the word *home* was all Layla needed to bury her face into Gethin's strong chest and block out everything else that she couldn't fix. She'd need her strength later. The next second that Gethin let his guard down, she would be up and out. And off for Nathanial, because maybe, just maybe, she would be able to take him away from his adoptive family before anyone else did. God only knew how she could ever forgive herself for ruining a seven-year-old's life, but a life on the run was better than death. Maybe she could even approach an angel for the first time and beg for help.

But for now she would enjoy the fleeting sensation that she was somehow safe in the hands that had just broken another demon's neck, and might end her life as well. Life sure had a wicked sense of irony.

"Where are we?"

At the alarm in her voice, Gethin looked up from the laptop balanced across his legs. Pushing fine strands of hair from her face, she blinked bleary eyes and realized that somehow, despite everything, she had managed to fall asleep somewhere after being carried out of the basement and long before she was put into the car she was now in.

"We're going to one of my properties." He shut the laptop with a quiet click and stowed it away, turning that taut, muscular body towards her. He had changed clothes, and was back in one of the tailored suits he tended to wear when doing business of the non-bloody kind. She was, confirmed by a quick scan, still in the same bloody, wrinkled skirt and blouse she'd been wearing the whole time, however long that was. Three hours? Five? Twelve? It was dark outside, so that meant at least nine, ten hours had passed since her glasses had been snapped. A lifetime away.

"Why?" The question that slipped out was a part of the longer question she wanted to ask—*why am I still alive?*

He ignored her, instead focusing on her bare feet. She looked down and winced at how swollen her ankle looked.

"I would have iced it had you told me," he chided.

"Can you make the swelling go down?" Layla asked hopefully. "You know, just shift my blood around or something?"

The blasted demon shook his head, not looking the slightest bit repentant. She tried moving her foot. It throbbed dully in response. "How am I supposed to get anywhere?"

The look he slanted at her was nothing short of ice. "Why would that be a concern of yours?"

She bit her lip. True, if she intended to sit docile and demure at his...his lair, then certainly, she could have every bone in her body shattered and it wouldn't matter. But she sure as hell intended to take off as soon as possible. "I want to be able to walk because I need to protect myself," she responded finally with every shred of dignity she could muster.

He turned his attention to the scenery flashing by, brightly lit storefronts and neon signs contrasting with shadowed streets and dark glimpses of the sky. "From whom, may I ask, do you need protection?" It was said in the same tone he might condemn someone to death, she decided. All arrogance and icy demeanor with something seething right beneath the surface.

"Because the air demons might break into your home and try to kill me."

He had the audacity to laugh. "You don't fear death. Remember? You've accepted your death is imminent at my hands."

"Well, maybe you won't torture me the way the air demons will." She said it softly, under her breath, but she could tell by the rigid set of his shoulders that he'd heard every single word.

"They won't get to you. They won't get to anyone I keep under my protection. No one knows you're here. Anyone who knows that you were locked away to begin with in one of the rooms will assume you're still in there."

The irony was too rich. "And we've established you can pick out traitors, haven't we?" Her bitter laugh strangled to a halt on a gasp of shock as he suddenly loomed over her, hands tight on her shoulders as if uncertain whether to shake or slide up and strangle.

"Don't remind me," he snarled. She watched in horrified fascination as the red of his eyes grew darker, deeper, and spread to slowly dominate his pupils until they were nothing more than a dying star among swirling pools of lava.

"I didn't mean to bait you," she whispered. To her chagrin, she realized the sensation tickling her cheeks were tears. Perhaps now was not the best time, but she had to ask. "How many—how many died?"

His hands slid away from her body. He didn't move back to his seat, instead remained too close for comfort. His harsh features seemed even sharper as he kept his face close to hers, gaze slashing across her face as if searching for the slightest hint of insincerity. He wouldn't find any.

"You might have saved Todd's life," he finally murmured.

"He's none too happy with you. Not only did the pretty office girl turn out to stab us all in the back, but she denied him a chance to protect his allies, and he shoulders the blame for the death of three friends."

Three. Three seemed like such a small number in the grand scheme of things, but that was three demons who had lived and laughed and maybe even loved. Three demons who died because of her, and she had no intention of asking for their names just yet. Call her a coward, but that knowledge she couldn't handle right now. All she could focus on was getting out. Out and away from a blood demon who held so much power over her, but left his intentions murky at best.

He reached out and touched her cheek, her temple, with strong hands lighter than a feather's stroke. The skin was sore and tender. Probably bruised where Vyn had struck her. That bastard.

"How did they torture you?" he asked.

"They didn't," Layla answered automatically. When she saw his eyes narrow she retracted the statement. "Well, they didn't make it pleasant. But I'm alive. I'd rather not discuss it." She realized belatedly that she was squeezing her hands together and made a conscious effort to keep them palms down on her lap.

She thought he was going to pursue it or make a dark comment about her limited time on Earth. She could see the words forming by the way he watched her with an odd combination of curiosity, anger and sarcasm. But whatever words were tethered on the tip of his tongue were swallowed back as he turned away to back into his side of the limousine.

She did her best to avoid the temptation of looking at him, dark and brooding, streetlamps illuminating the planes of his face in repetitive, violent flashes. She kept her gaze on her hands and forced herself not to shift uncomfortably whenever she sensed the weight of his gaze, and ignored the fact that her elevated heartbeat would be completely apparent. Damn him for bringing the torture up again and again. She was no stranger to deliberate pain—violence in her childhood and teen years was borne of alcohol and anger, slaps and scratches from her mother, the occasional backhand or shoves from the many men her mother brought home.

The violence under Vyn's orders hadn't been just deliberate, but methodical. No marks were ever left—scars on her body or too much damage to her mind would have been detrimental to their goals. Rather, it was emotional, it was magical and it was done to show her not only how vulnerable she was, but to showcase what would be done to her brother should she not succeed.

She had technically given the air demons what they wanted, but she was a loose end, and no one ever cared to trip over one. She would escape tonight, because there was no way Gethin would devote an entire night and day to babysitting her. The breach in security would demand all of his attention, and that would leave her to get past whatever guards he would put on her.

Except what would she do about her ankle?

The car rolled to a stop. Through her tinted window she saw they had reached a tall, thick wall with a heavily fortified gate that slid open smoothly a moment later. The car continued, slower now as the wheels crunched over gravel, and finally pulled to a stop in front of a mansion that probably had more in common with a high-tech fortress than just appearances alone.

"Go," Gethin said tersely. Without thinking, she opened the door and stepped out. With a gasp, she clung to the door to avoid falling as her injured leg sent a wave of dizziness and nausea over her. When her vision cleared of black dots Gethin's arms surrounded her.

Pride stiffened her back. "I can do it myself," she said, but then felt silly. Who was she trying to deceive? She couldn't, and the despair was another brick in the wall she felt was slowly and surely being erected around her, blocking her from what she had to do.

Gethin's eyes flashed in sudden anger and the arms around her tightened almost painfully until he gained control over himself. "I'm not going to carry you, you little fool."

It was as if Gethin seemed to understand and respected what little pride she had left. Despite their roughness, his words made her feel a bit better as she slowly made her way to the front of the house. The front door was opened by a demon who could have doubled for a linebacker. He spoke to Gethin, but focused a contemptuous glare on her. "Matthias just died from his injuries, sir."

Someone let out a small gasp of horror. Gethin's body was rigid, his pupils swallowed up in red, but the look in them was just as blank as the man's in front of him. "He did not die in vain, Marc. He'll be avenged. How many air demons were captured?"

"Twelve."

"How many of them are still alive?"

She remembered Gethin had snapped one of the demons' necks.

"Seven. What do we do with them?"

Gethin was quiet, and she searched his face anxiously. There wasn't an ounce of pity in his face, but she hoped. *Kill them quickly. Put an end to this gruesome war, please. Please.*

"I'm heading back for a few hours tonight after I handle her," he finally concluded. "Keep them drugged. We don't need them to play any of their damn asphyxiation games with us. Fucking exhausting."

She knew those asphyxiation games, and something of her thoughts must have shown on her face because Gethin turned the full force of his attention on her. "It's fairly exhausting for us to manipulate our own blood to increase the red blood cells and hemoglobin necessary to stay conscious. In attacks such as the one you witnessed, they can group together and really do damage. You, on the other hand, had no defenses, did you?"

She hadn't. Turning her face away from the all-knowing smile, she focused her attention to the austere interior of his living quarters. There was no sense of personality, of a warm household or relaxation. It was a building made for a warrior, one who valued survival over the luxurious trappings of a privileged life. She realized with a start that this was the way she'd lived. The simple decoration—admittedly, his probably cost twenty times more than hers—revolved around security. There were no large glass windows that would be difficult to defend, no frivolous furniture to inhibit movement.

Chances were it would be nearly as hard to get out as it would be to get in, but perhaps her handicap would also lure them into a false sense of security. She certainly hoped so, because the idea of grappling hand-to-hand with Marc wasn't pleasant at all.

As she studied the locks on the door they'd just entered, she realized it was quiet. Both men had stopped talking and were observing her with suspicious eyes. Hers widened in dismay. Did she have "escapee" tattooed on her forehead? To cover up her reaction, she blurted out, "May I have a shower, please?"

Marc's expression of distrust didn't flicker the slightest. Gethin's look, however, shifted imperceptibly. His nostrils flared, his jaw hardened and she was inexplicably reminded of his last words to her before he realized her betrayal—*You owe me a hell of a lot more than a kiss for this, and I fully intend to collect as soon as possible.*

Gethin must have sensed her heartbeat increase. He reached out to grasp her firmly by the shoulder. "I'll get her settled in. Once that's done, I'll leave and return in about three hours, four at the most. I expect her to still be here when I get back."

Marc addressed her for the first time, his voice cold. "Don't even try to run, whatever the hell your real name is."

"It's Layla," Gethin interjected, his gaze firm. "And I fully expect her to make a break for it. Your job is to keep her here without injuring her. Feed her too while you're at it."

The giant man didn't look too happy at the prospect of wasting food on her but nodded brusquely in acknowledgement of Gethin's orders. "I'll bring up something once you leave, sir."

Gethin's firm grip supported and guided her up two flights of stairs, though by the last one she was exhausted. Perhaps she should have swallowed her pride and let him carry her to conserve her strength. It sure looked like she'd need it, given that Marc was more than aware of her imminent jailbreak attempt. "Where am I staying?"

"In an extra room I have here." He steered her into one of the first doors on the third floor. Behind the dark wooden door that was probably more fortified than a tank lay a small bedroom with a queen-sized bed and connected bathroom.

"For how long?"

"As long as I say." He ignored the despairing noise she made. "And, so that you don't have any grand illusions of escaping, pick up this chair and swing it against the window."

"I don't have to," she murmured. "It's probably bulletproof, reinforced with wire and other things common human citizens such as I have yet to hear of."

"Accurate as always." He matched her quiet tone. "Now go into the bathroom and take your shower. I'll be back in—" He was cut off by the sound of his phone ringing. "Excellent." He brought the phone to his ear after glancing at the screen. "What did you find?" he asked, moving to the other side of the room to sit on the edge of the bed. She stood stock-still, hoping to overhear the conversation, but the volume was too low to make out any clear words. He caught her eye and made an imperious motion towards the bathroom.

She hesitated. Had it just been her imagination, or did she hear murmuring that sounded similar to her name?

He moved the phone away from his mouth. She saw instantly that his fangs had elongated. "If you don't get in there right now, I'm going to take it as an invitation to join you."

She obeyed as quickly as possible, slamming the bathroom door hard on the oh-so-masculine chuckle that followed tauntingly.

By the time she stepped out of the shower, she was not only bloodstain free, but apparently alone with nothing more than a towel. She had no desire to put back on her smelly, soiled clothing, but she felt helpless enough without being naked.

As lovely as the water had felt, it had hardly relaxed her or stopped her brain going a hundred miles per hour. There was no way she could escape, given that everyone in the building was on full alert. If only she were an angel or demon herself...then she could burst out of this house barely breaking a sweat, just like her favorite action-flick heroines.

She looked around the room, hoping to see something had changed since the last time she'd looked around—a sign for a hidden escape route, a phone or even a clock to check what time it was. All she saw was a bowl of steaming soup and a few slices of brown bread on the handsome dresser next to the bed. Next to it was a pile of clothes. Never one to turn her nose up at either, she dipped a piece of bread in the soup and stuffed it in her mouth as she wiggled into the man's shirt, socks and sweatpants. The top nearly swallowed her and the waistband of the pants had to be rolled up three times before it stayed, but the thick woolen socks were heaven-sent.

Heaven-sent. She dipped more pieces of bread in the soup and ate them slowly. She'd tried to pray for help before, when the demons had first confronted her and dragged her off, but she'd heard no response. How angry she'd been, that the angels hadn't even bothered to save her brother. Perhaps she wasn't going through the pearly white gates given the way she'd lived her life, but to not even help a seven-year-old?

It was worth a try. Just one more. Feeling foolish, she got to her knees, folded her hands and closed her eyes. "Dear...well, dear whoever's up there," she began hesitantly. "I know You probably get a lot of questions, given how the demons escaping from Hell has really thrown the entire planet into chaos, but if You can just get me out of here, I promise that I'll handle the rest on my own and that I'll save him. So, if You could do this for my brother..."

There was a long, awkward period of silence. She cracked open an eyelid, hoping to see something, but all that faced her was an empty room with a half-eaten bowl of soup. "Damn you all!" Layla exploded in anger and was getting to her feet when a sharp explosion of light enveloped the room, sending her back down to her knees. Half-blinded, ears ringing, she sat there motionless. Voices yelled in the distance and heavy footsteps pounded up the stairs. The door burst open a moment later and Marc, along with other men she didn't recognize, ran in with guns drawn. Layla moved out of the way and then made a soft sound of shock.

She was...glowing.

Chapter Five

"Where the hell did she go?" Marc bellowed. His gun swept around, pointed at her and moved away. Face contorted with rage, he didn't seem to see her at all. Nor did his men. "Fucking air demons!"

"But it was white, not blue. Only the angels have white light," one of his men protested.

"There's no way she's in league with the angels," Marc snapped back. "I'll notify Gethin. Call every man we have. We need to find her and bring her back in."

She sat there, too scared to move. Several men ran off as the rest ripped through the room, turning over the mattress and canvassing the bathroom. The glow on her skin, one that had hurt her eyes before, seemed the slightest bit...dimmer. She felt her adrenaline spike up. Clearly an angel had answered her prayer and was protecting her from detection. But how long would it last? Once the glow was gone, was that it? Given how fast it seemed to be diminishing, she had to move and fast.

Carefully getting to her feet, she quietly made her way out the room, hugging the wall as more men ran past her uttering guttural commands into phones and yelling curses mostly directed at her. She made it down the stairs and out the front door without triggering any alarms. Could they hear her? Her breathing quickened and her limping steps sounded overly loud to her ears despite the socks.

The driveway extended past gates opening to let out cars, and she aimed for it, knowing it was her only chance to get out of the compound. The road that lay outside the gates was deserted. It would be most prudent to cut through the woods parallel to the road. She could hitchhike once she became visible again. Gritting her teeth against the pain in her ankle, she marched off towards the line of trees bordering the road. As she plodded through the trees, finding a nice walking stick on the way, Layla sent a reverent and heartfelt thank you towards the night sky.

What had started off as a shiver had developed into a full-blown, bone-deep tremor. She couldn't feel her lips, but given the way her teeth were chattering she was lucky she hadn't bitten them to the point of bleeding yet.

Her skin had long stopped glowing, and the only roads she could find were devoid of cars. Humans stayed home at night nowadays.

She wondered where she was. Surely she should have seen a sign by now indicating what area she was in? The first house she'd buzzed for help after escaping was apparently empty. The second too. She rang, she pounded, she screamed and she begged. No one opened the door. Wary of the demons that were no doubt widening their perimeter with every minute she remained free, she opted to walk parallel to the road. No doubt Gethin knew of her escape. From how far away could he hear her heartbeat? From how far away could he smell her? Fear drove her farther and farther away from the highway, and now she was lost in the woods with nothing but damp sweatpants and sweater, soaked socks, a walking stick and a persistent, freezing drizzle to keep her company.

But she couldn't have walked that far, she reasoned. So if she walked at this extreme angle here, she would be able to...

"Get a grip, Layla," she told herself firmly. The hair stood up on her arms as if someone was watching her. Nervously, she looked around, but all she could see through the falling water were the dark, gloomy trunks of trees that seemed to hem her in from all sides. There were no strange sounds when she held her breath, just the pitter-patter of rain, a steady rustle of wind through leaves and her own harsh breathing when her lungs strained past the breaking point. Was it her imagination or was her blood racing more than it should be?

She forced herself to continue walking. One step, lean on stick, limp. One step, lean on stick, limp. One foot in front of another, head down, trudge on. She repeated this mantra, first whenever the mood struck her, then in her head constantly and finally out loud to distract her from her growing paranoia. At this point such suspicions were natural, and the stress clearly caused her to make irrational diagnostics about her surroundings. This scene was straight out of a slasher flick. Indeed, she was hunted by paranormal beings, but that didn't mean she was currently being stalked.

Then again, she hadn't survived as long as she had by ignoring her gut feeling.

Let's see. Hair standing on end? Check. Itchy feeling between shoulder blades? Yes. Elevated heartbeat? Not too uncommon by now, but yes. Goose bumps and nervous chills? She was getting pretty damn cold by now and her ankle was aching something fierce, but still, they were there, sweeping across her forearms and snaking down her spine.

A small flicker caught her eye and she spun around, raising her stick in front of her like it was a sword. Nothing. She stayed frozen, not even blinking, trying to take in the dark foliage around her, poised to flee at the slightest movement. Nothing moved.

Something crackled behind her and she moved too quickly to face the newest threat. Without the support of the makeshift cane, she stumbled on the uneven ground and wasn't able to catch herself as she fell hard on her rear end. There was nothing there, but she just sat there, gazing at the endless forest around her without actually taking anything in as despair began to eclipse rational thinking.

She had to face reality. Layla was terrified she'd waited too long. She was stuck in an endless forest with cold rain. Morning was hours away. She had no real weapon, no cash and no phone. She was injured, hopelessly outnumbered and couldn't find help, let alone the way back to the lesser evil she had to deal with. As much as it made her limbs feel leaden and lungs constrict, the only thing she could do for Nathanial at this point was to trust that Gethin would not be quite like the other demons. Perhaps if she could convince him that she could help him get revenge on the air demons somehow, he would promise to take care of Nathanial.

"Angel?" She queried softly, but she knew, just knew, that whatever had been with her for that brief second in Gethin's house was long gone. She needed to find a new way to keep going. But she couldn't. Not alone. She couldn't keep going, facing the entire world by herself.

"You won, Gethin," she said out loud, nearly gagging on the words. Louder, she screamed out, "You won! I'll come back. I'll stay with you. I can't go anywhere else." With what felt like a Herculean effort, she dragged herself to her knees, then to her feet. She'd walked in a fairly straight line, she thought. Perhaps if she tried walking back, she would find the road.

She turned around and felt her heart nearly stop.

Gethin stood there, black shirt plastered to his chest and hair in wet, curling tendrils, looking broader and stronger than the tree trunks he must have been hiding behind all this time. Her muscles tensed and adrenaline flooded her. Despite the pain in her ankle, she knew she'd be able to make a good run for it. But even as she took steps back, he didn't move a muscle. His eyes were calm. Both of them knew she wasn't escaping again.

"Nathanial's protected."

The words literally brought her to her knees and a sob rose in her throat. "Nathanial?"

He walked towards her, his pace unhurried. "Nathanial Alderman. Age seven. Birthday is next Wednesday. Nearly nine years ago your father traveled through the tiny town of Agnes, California. Nine months later, Nathanial Alderman was born, with no father listed on the birth certificate. Five years later you made a purchase on your credit card at a gas station near there. You did it again two months later. By then you must have learned he was indeed your brother. You probably use cash ever since then to avoid your transactions being tracked. You've worked for some pretty shady people in your past."

"I couldn't risk anyone using him as leverage against me." The words were hardly more than a soft sigh. "The couple who adopted him created a beautiful home for him. I could never forgive myself if I broke it."

"How'd the air demons find out about him?"

Shame coiled unpleasantly. "I...I check up on him. Around twice a year. Just to make sure he's being treated well, that he seems healthy and happy. It's a big enough town that I just play tourist. The air demons must have been tracking me as a potential spy, and... Well, let's just say that besides the hair, we could have passed as twins. I thought I was so smart with my secret, and walked back into my apartment to find a score of air demons waiting for me."

He crouched next to her, a rough hand pushing hair out of her face. "Did your mother tell you about a half-brother?"

"Once. She was drunk. I went through so many dead ends before I tracked down who I believe is the right child," she whispered. "But until there's a blood test, I can't even know for sure if he's my brother. How ironic is that? I'm going through hell for someone I've never hugged, never spoken to, someone who might not even be related to me. Does he have a bodyguard? Did you warn his parents? Is he frightened?"

He shook his head. "If he were older I would have spoken to him of the dangers he faces. I could always ask an allied angel to speak with Nathaniel's guardians, if that would make you feel better. But for now he has several rotating teams of blood demons constantly watching over him. We can hear the heartbeat of anyone approaching. We'll take care of him. I might be a demon, Layla, but—" his eyes darkened with chilling intensity, "—I am no child-killer. If you can only trust one thing I say, remember this—not all angels are good, and not all demons are bad either. In this war everyone is right. That's what creates war, after all. The demons are right to be furious at facing eternity in Hell with no chance of forgiveness. The angels are incensed at our freedom as we're just a bunch of sadistic, cursed bastards. And the humans are angry too, helpless and angry that they cannot see either side unless we will it. Except for a few like you who our sensory blocks don't work on at all." His hands radiated heat as they caressed her cheeks, her neck, her cold arms.

"How did you get out?" she asked. "I watch the angels and avoid the demons, but no one speaks of how you escaped. You speak of everything but that."

"I will never endanger your life by telling you secrets no human should ever know," he murmured with finality. "Though perhaps you are too deep in this already to be left in the dark. But you shall sicken if we do not get you warm soon. Will you protest if I carry you to my car?"

"Is it far?" she asked.

His eyes glinted with a sudden devilish mirth, and those lovely, firm lips turned upwards at the corners. "You would've never found that first road you were trying to walk parallel to. But there is an active highway about five minutes away in the direction you were already heading in."

She spluttered wordlessly for a moment, before tensions and terror dissolved into hysterical laughter. It had downgraded to hiccups by the time they reached the road. He put her down by a car parked twenty feet away. He pulled a heavy woolen blanket out of the trunk and wrapped it around her shoulders. "Before this gets too wet, strip out of those clothes."

She gaped at him for a moment. "No."

His eyes seemed to glow crimson for a brief moment. She shivered.

"I still could strangle you for escaping out of my house like that. You will explain everything to me once we get to a location where my men don't curse your name yet. Third one in two days. Biggest pain-in-the-ass human I've ever had the ill fortune to deal with. Are all human women like this? Get into the backseat and take off those wet clothes. Now. If you get sick I sure as hell won't play nursemaid. I'm taking you to my loft, and if you happen to destroy it somehow trying to escape again, I *will* kill you."

It was more his lack of desire for her to get sick than the threat of strangulation that persuaded her to strip down and surround herself with the blanket. Gethin got into the front seat and pulled smoothly away from the curb. The flannel was wonderfully warm against her chilled skin. The sound of her chattering teeth filled the interior of the car.

The initial warmth only lasted so long. The chill began to spread again, and her nose began to run. Miserably, she looked around for tissues, but found none. "Gethin, I need tissues pronto."

His irritated glare clashed with hers in the rearview mirror. "I don't have tissues. Use your shirt."

"That's disgusting," she muttered, but recognized it as the next best available thing and did so as discreetly as possible. She wrapped the blanket around herself tightly. "Can you turn up the heat?"

"It's up all the way."

"It's freezing!" she protested, but regretted her words a moment later when, with an ill-disguised curse, he jerked the steering wheel to the right to pull over sharply on the gravel. With a lithe twist of his body, Gethin maneuvered his way into the backseat with her.

"You're wet too," she warned breathlessly. His scent was all around now, dark and masculine, and she could see fangs protruding just a bit more than usual. His shirt was more damp than soaked by now, but there was no missing how the thin linen cloth clung to the dense muscles of his chest, the curve of his biceps. His eyes were darker, dark enough that the scarlet color could probably be mistaken for an odd brown should someone observe from far away. And there was no mistaking what burned in his eyes, what made his fangs slowly, elegantly elongate as her heart raced. Fear and desire were hand in hand when it came to Gethin, but she was finally going to let desire take control with no intentions of reining it back in.

"Are you going to bite me?"

He cupped her cheek in his palm and lifted it up and to the left, exposing the long, delicate line of her neck. His thumb brushed against her wildly fluttering pulse. "Scared? You should be," he rasped. "But first things first." He brought her face towards him, sliding two fingers between her parted lips. She hesitated for the briefest moment and then dragged her tongue across the slightly rough skin on his fingertips before snapping her teeth in a decidedly ungentle bite. His breath whooshed from his lungs with something akin to a snarl as he leaned over her and kissed her. His tongue entwined with hers, drawing out goose bumps of an entirely different nature.

He was slowly pushing her down until her back was against the car seats even as she arched her upper body towards his in an effort to press every inch of her aching body flush against his. The muscles, the sheer immovable, impenetrable wall of his body weighed on hers in such a wicked, erotic way that she wrapped her arms around his back and grabbed fistfuls of the material to drag him closer.

His hands had been braced on either side of her, but now he shifted his weight so that one hand gripped her hair, keeping her pinned down flat under him, and the other ripped at the blanket with a savagery he didn't even try to hide. Growling deep in his throat, Gethin tore at whatever cloth separated his body from hers. She tugged hard at the front of his shirt. The buttons gave way with little popping and tearing noises. He reared back momentarily on his haunches to fully remove the shirt, and as he lifted his arms to be parallel to the low ceiling of the car, all the hard, smooth expanses of silky golden skin she'd always fantasized about were there on display for her. She couldn't help but sit up too and run her nails across the waves of muscles that suddenly undulated across his chiseled chest. She wanted to see if he tasted just as smooth and hot and masculine as he smelled.

When all those lovely muscles bunched, she dragged her tongue across his chest and relished the oddly sweet and salty taste of his skin. She'd barely finished when his hands clamped over hers, raising them over her head to pin them against the seat. Bare beneath him, as if she were a sacrifice to a pagan ruler of the underworld, Layla struggled to breathe as she felt the tides of lust start to drag her under to the point of no return. Fear was a live flame, flickering and twisting in her core, but the heat only added to the razor edge she teetered on, and she knew which side she was going to jump to. So when Gethin opened his mouth, need hot in crimson eyes, she said simply, "Yes."

He pulled away from her embrace to study her face, traces of doubt still there on his. Desperate to get rid of them so that nothing else stood between them, she hooked her legs around his waist and pulled her body flush up against his, wanting his weight to press her into the cushions. She relished the masculine rasp of hair against her hardened nipples, the skin of her stomach, her sensitive thighs, the bare soles of her feet. The hard heat of him had her writhing against him, craving more.

"I won't stop after his," he warned her.

She answered by biting him.

At the sensation of her sharp little teeth, his self-restraint snapped and he tunneled his fingers through her thick, damp hair. A cry escaped her as he fastened his teeth against the delicate skin of her throat, hard enough that she froze, quivering. Her thighs gave way as he settled between them, rubbing his hardness against her slick folds, heightening sensitivity until she felt like a bow drawn taut. Yet she was too afraid to move, to demand that he do more, as the needle-like teeth stung her skin. She had her head pressed as far back as she could, but a part of her, wanton and wicked, wondered what would happen if she pushed against those teeth. If she let him taste her, take her in a way that no mortal ever could— such was the power he had over her.

She slowly leaned into it, and he pulled away with a snarl. "Not during your first time," he ground out. "Don't push me. You're not ready yet."

"But I want to," she demanded.

He responded by nudging the head of his cock against her entrance, and as she felt the broad, blunt head demand access she couldn't help but marvel at this—this man she held in her arms. Sculpted body shone golden with exertion, chiseled face with its set jaw and glowing red eyes, damp curls flush against his forehead—it was all hers, and hers alone.

And then he pushed in, and she thought no more. Pure sensation, of her being engulfed, filled, overwhelmed her. Her throat ached where he'd rested his fangs, and she could almost imagine the slide of teeth into her skin. His head was flung back, his breathing in time with his thrusts. She heard her own gasps match his, surpass his, become erratic as she lifted faster and faster to match his increasing thrusts. His hands held her head still, crushing his mouth to hers, tongue driving deep to assert dominance. She sank her nails into his back, marking him clearly. Damn it, she was so close, but each time she felt herself start to give into the pleasure he slowed down, taunting her, teasing her with the ultimate pleasure dangled just out of reach.

"Harder," she pleaded, and moaned as he suddenly pulled away, demanding hands around her waist, turning her over so that she was on her knees with her breasts against the seat. She could taste the sweat pouring down her face, hear the sound of flesh pounding, small growls emitting from his throat.

The throbbing heat turned white-hot, and she was dimly aware of her cries, full-throated as she surrendered gratefully to the orgasm that flashed through her body, leaving her exhausted and trembling in its wake. She felt his hips thrust erratically, felt him crush her hips to his as he thrust forth one last time, the long, hard length of him pulsing inside of her.

They stayed like that for a long time, until the heat that had fogged the windows of the car began to clear and their erratic breathing eased into one, slowing down. He gently turned her to her side, cocooning her against his hot body as she turned into his chest to wrap her arms around him, feeling, for the first time, utterly at peace.

"What now?" she mumbled, finally.

He chuckled into her hair. "Round two?"

"Shit."

His laughter was louder, longer, lighter than she'd ever heard it. "Don't tell me a little sex is too much for you to handle, Layla."

"One hour recovery, please," she retorted. "I'm getting sick after all. Don't want you to catch it—oh." She stiffened. "Speaking of catching—"

"No sexual diseases, thank you. I'm not *human.*"

She ignored his tone. "I was more referring to...other risks of unprotected sex."

"Can't impregnate you if you're fully human." When she looked up at him, eyes startled, mouth open to ask more questions, he simply leaned forward and kissed her until her eyes glazed over. "Maybe you're part demon, given that you can see us. You certainly bite like one. Which might be a problem, except the chances are slim to none, and I'd put all my money on the latter. Time for questions later—ones you're safe knowing the answers to, at least. But now that I've warmed you up, will you sleep?"

"Only if you hold me until then."

He did.

Chapter Six

She woke slowly, aware first of the silken sheets against her skin, and then of the warm body lying so near hers. She opened her eyes and looked directly into ones that were heavy lidded, wicked and more than a tad smug. "Good morning," she managed, aware her cheeks were bright red. A glance around told her that she must be in one of his apartments. Whereas the first one had resembled a fortress, this place looked like it had been plucked from the pages of an interior design magazine. Warm colors and deep browns melded together into one of the most luxurious bedrooms she'd ever seen in her life.

"Good morning, Ms. Layla Roads," he rumbled deep in his chest and stroked a possessive hand over her exposed breast. "I was rather hoping you'd wake up soon. I've plenty of things I want to do with you, one of which involves discussing your latest escape. The other deals with a repeat of last night, but with fangs." He flashed his, and she highly suspected that something else about him was erect right now as well.

"Which first?" she asked, feeling the delicious soreness of her body as she stretched. Her neck tingled as his words brought fantasies to life. How light she felt without the burden of Nathanial's safety weighing on her and the threat of death so far away. Gethin had made her safe again, but more than that, he made her feel...

No.

She was human. Mortal. He was a demon. Immortal.

And that was that.

As if sensing the sudden change in her emotion, his face went from playful to serious, the blank mask starting to slide back on. Her heart ached, a swift, hard yank that left her reeling.

"How did you escape from my house?"

"I'm not completely sure," she admitted, scooting back until she was half-sitting with her shoulders against the headboard. The cold metal reminded her of who—and what—she was dealing with. As seductive and delicious as he was lounging in the twisted bedding naked, under it all he was still an immortal killer who would never let emotion intercept with duty. "I...prayed."

His eyebrows went up. "I didn't peg you as the praying type, Ms. Roads. I assume you got an answer?"

"They've certainly never answered my prayers before, and I assure you there were plenty in behalf of Nathanial," she fired back. "My skin started glowing and no one else could see me." She remembered that bright explosion of light, the warm glow, and wished for the briefest moment that she could feel that again. As if she were safe and secure, but above all, loved.

"Odd," he mused. "That they would respond to you now. Though I suppose you escaping did force you to ultimately face that you need help. And here we are. I must remember to thank them when I see them again."

"Wouldn't the angels kill you on sight?" she queried. She remembered the few times she witnessed angels and demons coming together. The first time she'd seen such a battle, she'd wept when she watched an angel be overwhelmed and killed.

"Oh, Layla," he chided. "Haven't you figured it out yet?"

Layla was quiet for a long moment. "You're one of the good demons," she finally admitted, grudgingly. "Even though you enjoy assassinating everyone."

"Not everyone. Only nasty demons and humans who stuck greedy hands into places they shouldn't even know about." Lazily, he tugged at the sheet covering her. She tightened her grip and tugged back.

"Stop it, Gethin." She felt like throttling him. "All I could ever glean was that Vyn wanted to kidnap or kill someone before you did, and I'd appreciate it if you told me what the hell was going on."

"Not kidnap or kill," he chided. "That's only if she keeps running away from us. You have to understand, Layla, that we're all looking for this mysterious human someone because she did something no one should have been able to do."

"A *she*? And *human*?" She'd entertained the idea of mad scientists, demon kings on the run and traitorous angels, but whatever understanding she thought she had of the paranormal creatures was toppling fast.

"I told you human women are the most dangerous things I've encountered so far. For a bit I even entertained the thought that you might be the woman we're looking for."

"That I did what? What did she do?"

"She opened the portal between Hell and Earth."

There was a long, long silence while Layla gaped at him. Finally, in disbelief, she said, "That's what it's all about? Finding whoever caused this turmoil? I thought you knew and it was just a secret being kept from us humans. I can see and hear you guys, sure, but I had nothing to do with unleashing anyone. As far as my powers go, that's about it."

Gethin shrugged. "You can sense us no matter what safeguards we have, and you sure as hell are reclusive enough. For a while we had some intelligence swearing the woman who did so was blonde. Given that you were the first blonde I'd met with any kind of psychic capabilities, I couldn't help but wonder if the next cosmic joke would be fate dumping my target in my lap without warning."

"It was definitely a woman?" Her mind was spinning with possibilities. All the assassinations, tortures, blackmailing... It was no wonder every human, angel and demon was itching to get to the bottom of the mystery. Entire religions had imploded, crime ran unchecked in most cities, and more than one country had gone bankrupt when its citizens fled to more secluded areas in the world. Earth, as everyone knew it, was over forever. "Why are you telling me all of this?"

"Because if I thought you were a candidate after reading a background check on you, then others might as well. You should be prepared. But we've got a new lead. A brunette this time. You human women are such trouble, you know that?"

"She might not be human. She might be an angel. Or a demon."

"She's definitely part-human and has been on the run for five years straight ever since that portal opened up in the Nevada desert. Whoever she is, she has a lot of help and a lot of power." He shook his head, admiration obvious. "I'm working with the angels to get her, so that she can reseal the portal. Preferably with the more...mentally unstable demons on the other side."

"Why do the demons want her?"

"Depends which group you ask." He tugged at the sheet again, a frown on his face. "The demons who wish to have some kind of peaceful co-existence with the humans and angels just want to kill her so they don't get sealed away again."

"Oh, that sounds very peaceful," she snapped.

"Other demons want to use her power to break into Heaven. Get revenge for the millenniums they were imprisoned. It's bad enough we're on the saintly being's back porch. You can imagine they have no desire to let us in." He sneered. "So they asked me to do the dirty work for them."

"And what do you get in exchange?"

He was quiet for a long, long moment. "I get to stay on Earth, and never go back to that forsaken place," he finally whispered. "Before we escaped... Words cannot describe how we all existed down there. Born into war only to die in war. Imagine facing an entire life trapped in Hell, where loyalty and love are valued above all because there is so little of it. Nothing but endless treachery, betrayal and battle. And we're free now. It's a heady feeling. No one wants to give that up."

"Do you think the angels will kill the woman?" She felt anxious for the fate of this human. Surely it hadn't been intentional on her part.

"If they believe it's for the greater good, who knows? If she's half-angel instead of half-demon, it'll help her case a lot. Angels are extremely biased with that sort of thing. Just like humans."

"Well, of course we think demons are evil." She sounded more defensive than she meant to. Crap. She slid down the headboard and stared at the ceiling, trying to process all she'd learned. There were more people then. More people who had powers others didn't. "Crime isn't even documented anymore, it's so common. If demons aren't evil, who is?"

"Am I evil?"

"Well, no," she admitted. "You're trying to do good. I see that now."

He chuckled and rolled on top of her, letting his weight rest on her as he dipped his head to nuzzle the side of her neck. "Better hope I wasn't bullshitting you. Though one of the first things we learned when we broke free was how incredibly gullible human women are to a handsome face."

"I am *not* gullible."

He ducked the pillow she swung at him.

"You're emotional about me already, which is even worse. You won't survive long in this new world."

Her face burned at his charge, but couldn't deny it. She

didn't love him. She...cared about everything that was going on. Besides, if he wasn't the rampaging murderer she thought he was, why shouldn't she have some feelings towards him? It wasn't like anything would come of it. "There's nothing wrong with being emotional," Layla said stiffly. "In fact, I'd say I'm stronger for it. As for being emotional about you... I like you. I'm attracted to you. We had sex. It was fun. We might do it again. And then we'll go our separate ways. I'll go back to hacking computers and die in sixty or so years. I might even meet my brother when he's older. Maybe I'll get married and have kids myself. You'll live on and on until you're killed fighting demons. All by yourself. I think I have the better deal there." She felt tears sting and she turned away from him. "So now what do we do?"

His words were as cold-hearted as hers. "We can go our separate ways, as it seems that's all you want. You go back to your life, I go back to mine."

Too easy, she thought. "What about Nathanial?"

"What about him?"

"He needs protection from the air demons. He might need it for years."

"I don't work for free."

She felt the vises clamp in place, felt as if her freedom, once again, was slowly being strangled from her. "So I'm back to square one. What do you want from me?" Anger bubbled and boiled.

"You've got your life, so I really wouldn't call it square one."

"You're bargaining with my brother's life," she screamed. "How does that make you any better than Vyn?"

Judging by his involuntary flinch she'd struck a chord.

"Like I said, I don't work for free. I'm going to take a shower. You're welcome to join me when you're ready to discuss terms." Uncaring of his nudity, he let the sheets fall away as he strode into an adjourning room.

She waited until she heard the water running before marching into the bathroom. She whipped the curtain aside and turned off the hot water. Instantly gratified by the very un-demon-like yelp, she announced brusquely, "In exchange for my brother's long-term protection, I will help you find this woman, even if it takes many, many years. And when she is found, I want to leave this sordid life behind. Is that enough of a deal for you?"

Gethin turned the hot water back on and crossed his arms over his chest, water sluicing over the body she'd had over hers the night before. "I would have settled for your companionship, be it sexual or just friendship. But since you brought it up, I'll take your offer of assistance as well."

That was all he wanted? Had she hurt his feelings? Too bad. She ruthlessly squashed the ache in her heart at how lonely he'd seemed for a brief second. Like he said, being emotionally involved with any demon was just asking for trouble. "And once we find this woman we're through." She ignored the way her heart tightened at the thought of leaving him.

"If we no longer wish to be together, then yes." He tilted his face into the shower, running his hands through thick locks.

"I'm not immortal. I can't turn into an angel or demon either. I'm all human."

That seemed to amuse him. "Let's hope so. I didn't use a condom."

"But you're not bothered..." She hesitated, eyes searching his face for any sign of discomfort or pain. "Haven't you found that making friends with mortals is a bad idea because they all die?" *And what if I fall for you even more than I might already have?*

"Layla, I've only had the pleasure of being on the surface of this planet for five years. I've never been close to a human before, and I rather enjoy being with you, as perplexing as that is. I also have no intentions of ending this anytime soon. Do human women not hit their prime in their thirties? You're only at twenty-seven, after all. Wouldn't want to miss that."

Her mouth opened. Closed. Opened again. "I'm speechless."

"I'll certainly enjoy such a rare moment. Now, join me in the shower. Payback time."

Not fully comprehending what he meant, she let him pull her in and squealed when he pinned her against him and turned the cold water on full blast.

"We're one step closer now." Blood-red wine pooled at the bottom of the glass as Gethin tilted the bottle. The restaurant they were celebrating in was small, intimate and just what they needed after a long week of work. He wore his shades, as he always did when around humans, to hide his eyes. "Good call bringing in that portrait artist. Not the best, but at least we have some kind of a face to go on instead of just hair. Far harder to disguise."

Layla picked up a copy of the drawing. Big haunted eyes gazed up at her pleadingly. The woman looked to be around her age, with a delicate heart-shaped face and a bundle of chocolate curls spilling over her shoulders. Her lips were parted with surprise.

"She looks scared," she said softly.

"Can't blame her." Gethin nudged the wine a bit closer to her free hand. "She's got more hits focused on her than a network of terrorists."

"We need to save her."

Gethin made a noncommittal noise. "We'll see what her story is."

"I mean it, Gethin."

His legs squeezed hers under the table. "Layla, I will do my best to make sure everyone who deserves to stay alive does so. We've been over this a hundred times. Just because she's a fragile-looking female doesn't mean she—oh, hell. Who's calling me now?" Irritated, he checked the screen before shooting her an apologetic look. "I need to take this. Hold up." Before she could protest that the dinner was supposed to be stress free, he was striding away. Well aware that the women who had been ogling him all night were now openly staring at her, she focused on toying with the gnocchi on her plate.

Layla had been trapped before, but this was a different sort of trapped. She knew being with Gethin would cause her pain in the end, but she still kept going. She stayed with Gethin at one of his apartments and worked from there, tracking down the mysterious woman. But as she became more and more entrenched in this new world, she wished desperately to become a part of it. Each moment of happiness was bittersweet. She tried to cherish every second she spent with him, knowing well it couldn't last.

She'd fallen for the red-eyed demon, and she'd fallen hard.

A pity it wouldn't work out. It was only a matter of time before one of them had to move on.

She was startled from her melancholy when Gethin strode back in. "Something's up at the office. I need to go in."

"I'll go home."

"You don't go anywhere without me."

She glared at him. His protectiveness had been endearing the first week. Now she wanted to clobber him over the head to knock some sense into him. "Gethin, I cannot stay glued to your side for the next twenty years. You go to the office, I go home. I'll hop in a cab if need be."

"No. You're coming with me. Give it a few months, Layla. The air demons are still out there. No news is good news except when it comes to demons. We're only quiet when we're up to no good."

"And when you're not quiet?" she asked dryly.

He smirked. "That's when we're *really* up to no good." He efficiently tucked a few bills under his plate that more than covered the dinner. Without giving her much room to protest, he whisked her outside and bundled her into a cab. "I know you don't want to go back to the office, Layla. But just for a few minutes."

"I can't face them yet."

He didn't reply, but his hand closed around her, warm and strong.

Layla was quiet on the drive over and stayed behind in the lobby. She watched the elevator go up to the thirty-third floor and stay there. Nervously, she glanced around. There was no one here except for a guard at the reception desk. If he recognized her, he didn't let on. The minutes dragged on and on, and she was just about to call Gethin to ask him to hurry up when the elevator buttons lit up and began moving down.

The doors slid open and revealed a stranger, a tall, lean man with wraparound shades. She quelled her disappointment and looked away as the man stepped out. What was taking Gethin so long? She began to reach for her phone.

The man approached her cautiously, sliding the glasses down. "Layla?"

He looked vaguely familiar, and the red eyes proclaimed him a blood demon. He must have worked with her, spent time in the offices with her. Yes, she definitely knew him. Had he known any of the demons that had died? She sincerely hoped not. "May I help you?"

"Gethin asked me to escort you home." His face remained polite and friendly. If he hated her as much as she feared her old coworkers did, he hid it well.

"Damnit. Is he going to take much longer? I'd rather wait

for him." She checked her phone anxiously. It was nearing ten.

"A few hours."

She groaned. Far too long. "Oh, very well then. I'm so sorry, but I've forgotten your name. Rick, was it?"

He smiled. "Close enough. Richard." He stayed close to her side as they stepped out together onto the dark sidewalk. She felt something prick her arm, but there was nothing when she looked. A mosquito? As a cab pulled over near them, she felt her head spin.

"Richard?"

"Yes?"

"I don't feel well. Dizzy."

"Do you need help?"

She felt an arm wrap around her waist.

"You must have had too much wine. Here, get in."

Her heart was racing, her mouth cotton-dry. She felt herself start to fade as her legs sagged. Too much wine? She'd barely had a glassful, and if something had been wrong with it Gethin would be ill too.

Gethin. She needed to get to Gethin. But as she attempted to coordinate her movement, Richard's arms were banded around her. "You're going to pass out now for an hour, and when you wake up we'll be with Vyn," he whispered in her ear. "Gethin will be dead and the air demons will be *very* eager to see you."

The realization that she was being abducted came too late. The cab hadn't even pulled away from the curb before she was out.

When she came to, she was lying on a sofa with several demons standing guard over her. Richard leaned towards her.

"Well, hello there, princess," he drawled. "Guess I gave you a way bigger dose than I intended to. You've been out for almost eight hours. No matter."

Her heart was lodged so deeply in her throat it was a wonder she could breathe around it. She was in the nondescript, three-story brick house where she'd been taken prior to working undercover at Gethin's company. As she was unceremoniously hauled to her feet, one of the air demons opened the door and Richard shoved her through.

What could she do? Her skin crawled as Richard pushed her along down hallways and past rooms she remembered all too well. They were walking to the back of the house. Given what time it was, Vyn was most likely enjoying a light breakfast in the garden. He always had so relished simple human traditions.

When she stepped outside, it was to see Vyn leaning back in his chair, savoring what seemed to be an English muffin with chocolate spread on top. If she didn't know first-hand what he was capable of, she would have almost pitied him. Watching him, it was hard to ignore the truth behind Gethin's words about each side being right. If she'd been forever sentenced to eternity in Hell, and had been given a chance to escape to a place where she would not only survive but thrive, where would she have drawn the line to stay there?

Her heart hardened when he looked up and sneered. "Gethin can't care for you much if he let you slip away so easily. He's had eight hours to rescue you and still no sign of him. A pity he takes better care of your brother. We've been trying to kill the little brat for days now."

Fury took her breath away, but the burning desire for revenge gave her the strength to speak. "I cannot believe you would stoop so low as to kill an innocent child for revenge."

"You make it sound as if the death of a child is important in the long term." Vyn sighed. "You humans understand nothing of death and life, of what is unimportant and what actually matters. I must say, I've grown rather fond of your kind and the odd habits you've developed, but I'm afraid amusement protects strangers only so much.

"As for the information you obtained for us—I simply wished to warn Gethin's victims ahead of time. For the right price, of course. I'm very disappointed that you only got thirty-odd names for me. They were all—how should I phrase it—dead ends by the time I tracked them. Your demon lover has been quite the efficient killing machine. Until now."

"I didn't activate the emergency signal," she admitted, ignoring the fear that tunneled through her at his last words. "Another demon broke the glasses accidentally. I had no way to tell you to call off the attack."

Vyn's eyes flashed with annoyance. "It was the best emergency system we could come up with on such short notice. That certainly explains a lot. But, darling, if you don't mind—" he waved a hand in her direction, "—you've more than outlived your usefulness."

He'd barely finished speaking when she felt her lungs start to constrict. No oxygen. She tried to drag in one last breath before holding it, but there was nothing for her to breathe. She felt her vision blur and her lungs were stabbed with pain. She slowly sank to the ground as everything began to recede into nothing.

Abruptly, her next inhalation brought with it oxygen. Dizzy, shocked, she let herself lie on the cool stones of the garden. Vyn's voice came from somewhere above her. "Ah, don't die quite yet. I've a scout coming back in a few minutes, one who swore he'd bring your brother back to me. Another traitor from Gethin's men, actually. My, my, is he having a bad day."

Everything was terribly, horribly wrong. Surely the breaches in security weren't so bad, were they? A slash of light appeared and widened enough to let a lone figure step out with no little boy in sight. "Gethin," she breathed. How on earth...

"If one person even thinks of moving, they're dead." Gethin's voice was cold. "My men have surrounded this place, and it is up to you whether or not you want to die painlessly."

Vyn leaped from his seat, hands clutching his face, his throat, his stomach as he began to bleed.

"Mercy!" Vyn cried out.

"The same mercy you showed Layla and her brother? The same mercy you show any of your victims? I'm no angel. Such words won't change your fate. But if you let Layla go free now, unharmed, I shall tell my men who have just circled off your entire block to kill quickly and with mercy, as you so like to call it." He looked at Layla, his mask slipping. "I realized too late that phone call was a trap. Step through the air portal, and don't mind the dead demons on the other side. It's perfectly safe. The demons who are still alive aren't traitors."

She hesitated, looking at the bleeding air demon. He'd tortured her, intended to torture her brother, but seeing him dripping blood onto his neatly set table for one, she felt sadness wash over her. She wouldn't mourn him, not at all. Nonetheless, it was heartbreaking that peace negotiations of some type couldn't be settled upon.

"I'm not strong enough to fight in these battles," she admitted.

"Someone I care for told me emotions weren't a weakness, Ms. Roads," Gethin reminded her. "Off with you. Justice must be served with as much compassion as I suspect you feel. And when this is over, I shall do my best to replace these past weeks and months with new memories. Your role in this war has ended with Vyn's death."

Tears falling, she stepped through the air portal without looking back, knowing full well that every air demon in that house would be dead in the next minute, and with them, the knowledge of her brother's connection to her and thus Gethin.

Her part was over.

Gethin had taken a month off, but he couldn't spare more than that. For four long, glorious weeks, he made good on his promise to her—that whatever time they may have together, they'd make the best of it. But three days ago, work had come with a vengeance. He'd returned with semi-permanence to the office, and she stayed at his condo.

"Come meet me at work," he invited. "Lunchtime. Take a break from the computer before your eyes melt. I haven't seen you in two days."

She rubbed a hand over her face, even as his voice ignited a slow, warm glow inside. After so many weeks spent exclusively with him, the first few days back into the normal rhythm of things was difficult. "I can't." When her answer was met with silence, she sighed. "I can't go back there and face everyone. Not after...not after how I left."

"They forgive you. They understand."

"Even Todd?"

He hesitated. "Todd is on shift guarding Nathanial. But no, Layla, I think a part of him can't forgive you until he forgives himself. He was close to you and close to one of my demons who died. But if you're not ready yet I'll see you when I get home. I'll bring dinner. Pick your poison."

"Cheeseburger."

He snorted.

"There's a gym here, thank you very much. I'm just craving a burger. I'm stressed. You've given me an impossible target to track down. If it weren't for those confessions you got, I'd say this woman died at twenty and that was that."

"Except we all know she's alive and kicking. I want another step made in this case by Thursday." He hung up the phone.

She was nuts about the damn demon, and they both knew

it. He cared for her too. It was an unspoken rule that neither brought it up because the mere idea of anything permanent hurt. In the weeks they'd spent together after Vyn's death he'd opened her eyes to a whole new world, telling her all about demon and angel lore, stories of where he came from and what it had been like. He still refused to tell her parts of it, though whether it was because he worried for her safety or because it was still too painful, she didn't know.

Hanging over the relationship was the knowledge that it would end for her as she grew old and he didn't. She knew instinctively that he would be there for her as long as possible. Even so, she feared anew for his life, that a battle or accident would rip him away from her. But he must suffer doubly so— not only was she physically less strong should something happen, but there was time. Always ticking, always passing, as she grew older and older with each passing day while he stayed the same. She'd teased him about it once, but he hadn't laughed.

She was being silly, she scolded herself. Being gloomy about something that would happen in ten, twenty years. Resolutely, she pushed the worries out of her mind and focused back on the task at hand, determined to finish it long before the deadline he'd set.

True to his word, Gethin picked up the dinner she wanted. She smelled the food even before he came into view. Turning away from her computer, she leaped up and flung her arms around him as he walked into her office space she'd set up in the corner of his home office.

His body went from warm and gentle to distant in a heartbeat.

Worried, she pulled back. "Are you okay?"

He stared down at her, eyes narrowed. A muscle ticked in his jaw. "There's someone else here," he stated harshly. His eyes were growing darker and darker with each passing second.

She took another step back, wrapping her arms around herself. She was suddenly chilled to the bone as she glanced around nervously. "What do you—" She stopped in shock as Gethin knelt at her feet, pressing his face into her stomach. "Gethin. What on earth has gotten into you?"

"There's a heartbeat," he rasped. The look on his face when he pulled back and looked up at her nearly broke her heart. "Layla. There's another heartbeat."

It took a moment before it sank in, and then she simply fell back into her chair, bringing them to similar heights. "You said that's not possible."

"No, I said that demons could only impregnate angels and other demons."

Her smile wobbled. "I'm no angel. Or a demon, for that matter."

"Current data proves otherwise. You must have an ancestor, somewhere down the line, responsible for this." He laughed, sounding as shocked as she must have looked. "Of all the humans on the planet, I found the one who's got immortality in her blood."

"I'm not wholly human." She leaned forward and rested her head against his sturdy shoulder, wild elation coursing through her. She was pregnant. She carried his child. It must have happened the first time they'd made love. So many possibilities, a whole new life had suddenly opened up. She trembled.

"I would have never guessed..." He trailed off. Lifting her face in his hands, he examined her deeply. "Layla. I will always, always be there for you. And our child."

"I know," she whispered. "I just never thought that this would happen. Ever."

"But it did." He took a deep breath. "And while I may not have planned it this way—I wouldn't trade this for the entire world. We'll take this one step at a time, you and I. How do you feel?"

"Surprised," she said, attempting to smile. "Happy. Confused. Excited. A bit nauseous."

He laughed deeply. "You'll be one of those hanging over the toilet every morning then, will you? Fuck me. If someone had told me a hundred years ago that I'd be in this position with someone I...someone I loved, I would have killed them for taunting me with such hope."

"You love me."

"Didn't I just say that?" He actually bit his lip.

Laughter spilled out. "And you called me the emotional one. God, Gethin. I love you, though I'm sure you've figured that out already."

Reverently, he placed a hand over her stomach, and she ached to hear what he clearly could. "Perhaps miracles do happen, after all."

Smiling so widely she felt as if she could explode with joy, she laid her hands over his on her abdomen. "Yes, Gethin. They do."

About the Author

To learn more about Tarra Blaize, please visit www.tarrablaize.com. Send an email to tarra.blaize@gmail.com

Deals with Demons

Victoria Davies

Dedication

To my amazing family, who has always loved and encouraged me.

I couldn't have done this without your support.

Chapter One

"The master has ordered you home."

Talia tipped her mug up, savouring the last mouthful of beer before she slid the empty glass to the waiting bartender.

"Bully for him," she told the unwelcome man perched on the barstool beside her.

"I'm to bring you home at once."

Slanting a glance at the nervous man, Talia smiled her most vicious grin. "You can try," she replied, twisting her body to show him the glint of the dagger strapped to her waist.

The man gulped.

She shook her head in disgust. He was a disgrace. Why had Devlin even bothered to send him?

"You can tell your *master* he is welcome to try and force me back. But it will take a braver man than you to get me there."

Talia slid off the stool. She stalked through the crowded bar without a backwards glance.

Once outside she pulled her black coat tightly around herself to ward off the chilly night air. A single thought burned in her mind as she set off in the direction of her modest apartment. Why did Devlin want to see her after all this time?

Talia had been nineteen the night she fled Devlin's mansion. Not once in the six years since had he tried to contact her. And she'd know. She'd been waiting for him to make his move practically from the moment she'd left. The fact that he'd never come for her merely underscored what she'd known all along. To Devlin St. Clair she was not, and never had been, of any importance.

So why did he want her now?

She picked up her pace, trying to run from the unwanted memories.

Two things were special about Devlin. The first was simple. She'd been utterly in love with him since she was sixteen. The second was far more unusual. Devlin was a demon. As if that weren't enough, he also happened to be the most powerful demon in the city. Some might even argue the country.

The world Talia lived in was very far from the one most people thought they knew. Her life revolved around blood, death and magic. It had since the night her family had been murdered when she was fourteen.

Talia shook her head to try and repress the memories. It had been a night much like this one when her life had changed forever. The nip of autumn hung in the air and overhead the bright moon was almost full. She'd been in her room when the demon broke into her home. Her parents' screams had woken her. Because of her rather unusual talents, she'd known immediately what was in her house and she'd known which way he would turn when he climbed the stairs and reached the landing. Her room was to the right of the stairs, her younger brother and sister's was to the left. Talia had thrown herself out the window with the sound of the squeaky floorboard in the left hallway echoing in her ears. Saving herself had torn her apart, but she'd known, even then, she was no match for the demon. Unable to do anything else, she'd run until she was too exhausted to move.

And there Devlin had found her. Huddled in an alleyway, Talia had been trying to hide herself behind a garbage can when he rounded the corner. She'd known what he was, of course.

She always knew. But unlike the monster in her house, this demon had crouched before her and silently held out his hand.

"I swear, child, I will never harm you," he'd whispered to her. He said nothing else, merely waited. Eventually Talia had crawled forwards and put her dirty hand into his.

In one night she'd lost everything she'd loved and gained a new life unlike anything she'd ever imagined.

Devlin had brought her to his mansion on the outskirts of the city and she'd lived there for five years. He'd found her the very best tutors to teach her since he refused to let her go to a normal school. And after her academic classes he trained her himself in all varieties of combat styles. Thanks to him she was one deadly woman. But he'd done more than train her. Devlin had been the first person to explain what she truly was.

Talia was a senser. She was gifted with the ability to feel demons and anticipate their movements. Those were the skills that had saved her life when her family had been attacked. Sensers' abilities made them unparalleled trackers and, given how rare a true senser was, their skills were in high demand. Capitalising on her gifts, Talia quickly made a name for herself as a demonic bounty hunter after she left Devlin. After all, a girl needed to eat and her former benefactor had kindly given her the training needed to hurt all the things that went bump in the night.

Which brought her back to why Devlin was looking for her in the first place.

He couldn't have been happy to learn he'd personally trained a woman who earned her bread by killing members of his race. However, if he wanted retribution he was a little slow. She'd been doing this for six years, and with his resources there was no way he'd be unable to find her if he truly wanted to.

Talia drew up in front of her apartment building and fished for her keys. With her salary she could afford a much nicer place, but this apartment was convenient and she liked its old charm.

She hopped into the warmth of the entrance way, thankful to be out of the chilled October air. There was an elevator in her building but she jogged up the stairs instead. An out-of-shape senser was a dead one. Five flights later she turned the keys in her door and entered her haven.

The apartment might not be sprawling but she'd filled the small space with absolute luxury. Her home had all the state-of-the-art toys. A huge flat screen TV hung on the wall before the most comfortable leather sofa Talia had ever felt. Her kitchen was equipped with all the fixings, even if she rarely used them. Takeout was more her style.

Talia kicked off her shoes and headed for her large bedroom. A massive king bed dominated the room and, with a loud sigh, she dropped backwards onto the soft mattress.

Closing her eyes, she relaxed into the bed.

By now the henchman had probably reported her words to Devlin. She wondered if he would actually come for her himself or if he would merely shrug and turn his mind to other matters.

Wincing, she acknowledged the latter option was far more likely. While her world had once revolved around Devlin, in his world she was merely a decoration. His pet senser.

Sitting up, Talia looked across the dark bedroom at her vanity mirror. She had changed since they last met. The skinny teenager had filled out into a nicely curved woman. Her once long black hair was now short and red. The pastels she'd favoured had been replaced by a full wardrobe of black. The only thing the same was her icy blue eyes. Well, she amended as her gaze dropped to her throat, her eyes and the black rose forever embedded into her skin.

The outline of a rose in bloom was clearly visible over her jugular. Right where Devlin had bitten her. At the touch of his lips, the small symbol had stained her flesh, never to be removed.

Demons are not vampires. They don't need to drink human blood to live, but for some demons as old as Devlin, blood could be an irresistible temptation. It was like adding brownies to a chocolate sundae. Not necessary but sinfully delicious.

Seeing the mark on her throat filled her with shame. Memories of the night she'd fled Devlin swirled in her mind.

As a child, it had taken Talia the better part of two years to fully trust Devlin. He'd been forever patient with her, waiting for her to accept him for what he was. But once she had been able to put aside her fear of the fact he was a demon, she had no defense against the other emotions he inspired. At sixteen, he had been an irresistible fantasy. Endless nights had been wasted fantasising her demon would sweep into her room and declare his undying love. Unfortunately for Talia, as she'd grown so had her feelings for her tempting demon saviour. She remembered waiting breathlessly on her eighteenth birthday, wondering if now he'd finally see her as a woman instead of a child. But Devlin was never short on bed partners and when his choice of companions tended to be tall, perfect models it was hard to compete.

But everything had changed a year later, on her nineteenth birthday.

Talia squeezed her eyes shut.

That night Talia had lost her virginity and her home. Again.

"Don't come looking for me, Dev," she whispered to her dark room. "Let me disappear."

Chapter Two

The night air felt cool against her heated skin. Beyond the balcony rail the city glittered in the darkness. Talia fidgeted with the hem of her light pink strapless gown that had been carefully chosen to show off her creamy skin and long legs. Here's hoping it helped her win her birthday wish.

"I found another bottle," Devlin said, stepping onto the balcony.

Talia twisted in her chair to see him. No matter how much time she spent by his side, she would never get used to his stunning looks.

Towering over six feet, he was not a man any fool messed with. His long blond hair was pulled back from his strikingly beautiful face. Piercing green eyes studied the wine in his hand as he absently walked over to her. Tonight he'd forgone his usual black suits in favour of simple slacks and a tight black silk T-shirt. Watching the way the material molded to his chest, Talia unconsciously licked her lips. Even dressed casually, Devlin was a man who took her breath away. How had she managed to live with him for five years without jumping him?

Well, no more, she decided, eying him hungrily. Tonight was her nineteenth birthday and all she wanted was him.

Devlin dropped into the chair beside her and set the wine bottle next to the half-eaten birthday cake on the small table.

"How does it feel to be nineteen?" he asked with a smile.

"Much the way it felt to be eighteen," she replied nervously, wondering how to phrase her request.

Devlin, it's my birthday. Do me. She sighed. Not quite the sophisticated offer she wanted. Besides, she was crazy to even imagine he'd want to be with her. She saw the women he dated. Hell, his harem lived in the mansion most of the time. There was no way for an awkward nineteen-year-old to compete with the elegant models he preferred.

"You're thinking too hard," Devlin told her, opening the wine and pouring them each a glass. "I can see the little wrinkle you get on your forehead."

Talia touched her face self-consciously. "You can't," she denied.

"What were you thinking of?"

"Birthdays," she said with a sigh.

"Yes, because you are getting so very old," he teased.

She supposed for a man who'd lived centuries, a nineteenth birthday was nothing at all. But she was mortal. The best she had to hope for was another five or six decades with him. Every year mattered.

"I haven't gotten you a birthday present yet, have I?" Devlin mused. "What do you wish for your birthday, Tali?"

"You," she blurted without thinking. Talia winced. It hadn't been the smooth, seductive invitation she'd imagined. When she peeked at Devlin she saw he was frozen with an unreadable look on his face.

Dammit, she thought, a blush heating her cheeks. How did she undo this blunder?

"What do you wish for your birthday?" he asked again, slowly.

Talia sucked in a sharp breath. Was he serious? She'd spent enough time around demons to understand the basic tenants of magic. To bind a wish you had to answer it three times. He was taking her seriously.

"You," she whispered, unable to look away from his eerie green eyes.

Moving faster than Talia could see, he appeared before her, crouching on his knees. "Careful," he warned her. "Only one more chance. Have a care with your answer, Talia, for if you bind this wish I won't let you go. What do you wish for your—"

"You," she cut in.

Devlin swept her into his arms before she'd even finished the word. One hand tangled in her long black hair, tilting her head up. Devlin met her eyes, hesitating a moment before he lowered his head and claimed her mouth.

Talia gasped as he kissed her for the first time. How many nights had she imagined being in his arms? And now she was. Before the night was finished, she'd be a demon's lover.

Her hands gripped the chair arms uncertainly as he kissed her. His intensity was overwhelming. She struggled to match his passion but Talia didn't exactly have much experience to draw from. She'd been in love with one man all her life. Dating boys her age had never seemed very appealing when she compared them to Devlin.

"Open your mouth, darling," he murmured against her lips.

Parting her lips for him, Talia gasped as his tongue touched hers. She wanted this, she did, but suddenly everything was moving too fast. She couldn't find her footing.

Gasping for breath, she pushed the demon back and jumped to her feet.

"Dev," she panted. "Wait."

Slowly, Devlin rose before her. His eyes glowed with an inner fire and the sight sent a shiver of delight racing down her spine. A demon's eyes glowed in situations of intense attraction. At least she knew he truly wanted her.

"I told you," he murmured, waltzing her backwards until

she hit the brick wall of the mansion, "I'm not letting you go."

"I'm not asking you to," she said breathlessly.

He stepped forwards, pressing his body against the full length of hers. When his knee parted her legs, she clutched his shoulders for support.

"I've waited so long for you," he told her, cupping her face in his hands. "Don't be afraid."

Twisting her head, she laid a gentle kiss on the palm of his hand. "I could never fear you," she whispered.

Devlin closed his eyes as he leaned his forehead against hers. She made no protest, revelling in his closeness. The way he held her soothed her trepidations. Devlin touched her as if she were something infinitely precious to him. How she wished she truly was. Maybe tonight was their new start. She'd make him fall as deeply in love with her as she was with him.

When he opened his eyes, Talia read only tenderness in them.

"Come inside with me."

Talia swallowed hard, managing only a shaky nod.

Stepping back, Devlin caught her hands and pulled her with him. He led her slowly to the entrance to his bedroom and slid the glass door open.

Talia glanced back at the birthday cake and bottle of wine. She wished she'd thought to have an extra glass for courage.

"Your choice," Devlin told her. "It's always your choice."

She knew that. For all he was a demon, she knew he'd never hurt her in any way. There was no one she trusted more than him.

Tentatively, she placed her hands on his shoulders and pushed him backwards.

His room was dark. Only the weak moonlight streaming through the floor-to-ceiling windows illuminated the massive space. But she didn't need light. She knew every inch of the mansion, including Devlin's personal domain. He had never restricted anything from her.

Which meant she knew exactly where the decadent king-sized bed lay.

The door slid closed behind her, moved with invisible hands. Talia never flinched. She was used to being around demons working magic.

Devlin walked backwards, his gaze never leaving hers, until he stood before the bed.

Unable to tear her gaze from him, she forgot to breathe as she watched him slowly grip the hem of his shirt and pull it over his head. She'd seen him bare-chested before but never under such exciting circumstances.

He tossed the shirt away before running his fingers along the fastening of his slacks. Talia held her breath as he hesitated, toying with her. With a crooked smile, he finally unzipped the pants and let them slip over his hips. He kicked the material away, but Talia didn't even spare the discarded clothing a glance. Devlin had just revealed he wasn't the kind of demon to wear underwear.

Talia sucked in a sharp breath as she looked at him naked for the first time. There was nothing soft about Devlin. His body was as honed as a blade. It was made for power and strength. And yet tonight it would be capable of bringing pleasure as well.

He let her look her fill before raising a hand to her.

"Come to me," he commanded.

Talia had no choice but to obey.

She walked to him, trying to hide her nervousness. There was no denying she was in over her head. When she slipped her trembling fingers into his, he pulled her into his arms. He kissed her thoroughly, drawing his lips over hers. Talia tried her best to match his passion but she lacked the experience she needed to truly bring him to his knees.

"Relax," he murmured, answering her groan of frustration. "There will be other nights, my daring girl. Tonight is for you."

"But I want to be good for you," she confessed in a humiliated whisper.

Devlin laughed painfully. "Tali, nothing about you could ever disappoint me. If you want to learn—" he drew his lips over hers, "—I am more than willing to teach. But it would only be refining your natural skills."

"What skills?" she groaned.

Devlin dropped a light kiss on her exposed shoulder. "You destroy me," he whispered to her. "No one else has the power you do."

She drew a sharp breath at his words. Biting her lip, Talia reached behind to grasp the zipper of her dress.

"Teach me," she told him, drawing down the zipper.

Devlin watched with hot eyes as the fabric parted and fell away. The dress had been too tight for a bra and Talia stood before him in only her skimpy black panties. Rolling her shoulders back, she stood tall and waited for his verdict.

"You are so incredibly perfect," Devlin murmured, his eyes glowing brightly in the darkness.

Talia released the breath she hadn't even realised she'd been holding.

Grabbing her around the waist, Devlin grinned wickedly. Before she could protest, he tossed her backwards onto the bed.

"Warning next time," she grumbled, trying to sit up.

Devlin dropped onto her before she could move. He caught her wrists and pinned them above her head with one powerful hand.

"Mmmm," he murmured, looking down at her. "Delicious."

She laughed nervously. "Is the big bad demon going to eat me?"

His eyes glowed brighter. "Your wish is my command."

Devlin ran his lips down her throat and continued to slide down her torso. Talia gripped the black sheets, riding the incredible sensation of his touch. She barely noticed when he pulled her panties down her legs. But she did notice when his fingers trailed slowly up her inner thigh.

"Devlin!" she gasped, reaching to push away his hand.

A delighted chuckle rumbled from him. "Enjoy," he told her, moving up to kiss her quickly.

Talia eyed him dubiously as he reached out to run the tips of his fingers up her legs. Her breath caught at the shocking sensations such a light touch inspired. Devlin's hot mouth trailed over her body, finally pausing when he reached her breast. Rolling his eyes up so he could see her, he took one pink nipple into his mouth. Talia cried out as pleasure shot through her.

"Devlin," she groaned, trying to navigate the new sensations.

As he suckled her, he drew his fingers higher and touched her lightly between her thighs.

"Oh my," she gasped as a single finger traced her folds. "That can't be legal."

"Little innocent," Devlin murmured, sliding back down her body. "You told me to eat you, remember?"

As his head slipped down between her legs, she realised what he intended. "I didn't mean...ah..." she moaned as his tongue replaced his fingers.

Talia arched off the bed with a ragged cry. She twisted in the sheets as her demon lover played with her. Never in her wildest dreams had she imagined anything like what he did to her.

"Dev, stop!" she finally cried when she couldn't take it anymore.

With a last lick, Devlin raised his head. Overwhelmed by

the pleasure, Talia could only stare mutely at the smiling Devlin. His expression was filled with pure male satisfaction as he climbed up her body.

"Ready?" he asked wickedly, licking at her breast.

"Oh my God," she gasped.

"Come now, darling, you don't have to call me that. I'll also answer to 'my master'."

Talia laughed, hitting him on the shoulder. He retaliated by squeezing her nipple, making her writhe beneath him.

When her pleasure-fogged mind cleared enough for conscious thought, she cupped his face between her palms and kissed him softly. "I'm ready," she told him.

Wordlessly, he shifted to fit himself against her entrance.

"Hold on to me, sweetheart," he told her, pressing forwards.

Talia gasped as he forced his long length into her. Pleasure disappeared in the wake of a painful pressure building within her.

"I changed my mind," she cried.

"Hold on, love," he replied, stopping. "Just a little more and I swear I'll make it all better."

Talia eyed him warily, biting her lip, but slowly nodded.

Gritting his teeth, Devlin thrust into her.

Talia screamed, arching off the bed. "Oh hell!" she yelled, battering his shoulders. "I don't know what the other women told you, but trust me, they lied. You are so not good in bed."

Devlin groaned, striving to hold himself perfectly still. "It's only like this the first time," he assured her.

"Dev, if you think there'll be a second time you are one seriously delusional demon."

Devlin shook his head in exasperation before leaning down to stop her flow of words with a kiss. With his free hand, he played with her breasts, sending spikes of pleasure through her to make her forget the pain. Talia willed her tense body to relax.

Already the pain was fading, leaving behind the foreign feeling of invasion.

"Better?" he asked her, his voice strained.

"A little."

Devlin groaned in relief and carefully shifted inside her.

Talia gasped in surprise at the pleasure she felt.

"Much better," he purred, seeing her reaction. Slowly, he withdrew.

Watching her wide eyes, he slid into her again. Unlike the first time, Talia felt no searing pain. Instead, a curious heat spread through her.

"Again," she commanded, wanting to test this unfamiliar pleasure.

Grinning, Devlin complied. He rocked into her leisurely, giving her time to adjust to his presence. When her body started to relax around him, however, he picked up the pace.

"Lift your hips," he commanded, pulling her up to meet his thrusts.

Talia threw back her head, moving her body as he commanded. Every time he drove into her she felt a pressure building within her. But this time, it wasn't uncomfortable. Every thrust broke a little more of her control. She dug her nails into his shoulders, trying to ride out the waves of unfamiliar pleasures pounding through her body. She rocked her hips instinctively, matching his rhythm.

Any thought of pain was long gone from her mind. Instead, all she felt was tortuous heat.

"More!" she cried, not even realising what she was asking for.

Devlin drove into her, pushing her closer and closer to that precipice within her.

"Devlin," she gasped as he thrust into her one last time and pushed her over the edge.

Talia screamed as her climax rocked her. She'd never felt anything like the pleasure that swamped her. Every cell in her body exploded at the same time. The world blacked around her as she tried to cling to consciousness.

She heard Devlin above her cry out and felt a piercing pain in her neck. Her demon lover had sunk his sharp fangs into her throat. The thought might have disturbed her before, but right now it only added to the pleasure. Her orgasm continued as he drank from her, battering her with unending waves of indescribable pleasure.

Finally, Devlin drew back his head.

Talia stared at her lover and watched a single drop of her blood trail down his chin.

Talia jerked awake, falling less than gracefully from the bed. On hands and knees, she scuttled backwards until she hit the wall.

Her harsh breathing filled the dark, empty room. She was alone.

"It was a dream," she said aloud, trying to calm her racing body. "Only a harmless dream,"

Maybe thinking about Devlin had stirred up the memories of their one time together.

Talia reached up to touch the black rose on her throat, half-expecting to feel an open wound. But the skin was smooth and blood free. It may have been a freakishly realistic dream but it was a dream none the less. Devlin was not here. She was no longer nineteen. And she was not the silly woman who'd once loved him more than anything.

Talia was older now, and wiser. She'd never fall into the old trap of thinking Devlin gave a damn about her. He was a centuries-old demon, after all. Manipulating people was a hobby for him. It was her fault she'd believed the magic of her nineteenth birthday meant as much to him as it had to her.

She pushed herself to her feet before stumbling back to the bed. Devlin St. Clair was no longer her fairytale hero. If he knew what was best for him, he'd stay the hell out of her way.

Chapter Three

A demon lounged against her building.

Talia had spent her night tracking a rather pitiful mark trying to escape his overlord. All she wanted to do was take a long, hot bath and sleep like the dead. But instead she had to deal with the freaking demon in her path. Who did a girl have to kill to get a break around here?

With a sigh, she strode forwards. Talia was not a woman who ran from her fears. At least not anymore.

As she came closer she noticed two unusual things. The demon stood deliberately in the shadows to hide his face and, beyond the fact that he wasn't human, Talia couldn't sense anything else about him. Usually she felt demons' emotions and could predict their movements. Sometimes she learned even more, sensing ages, desires and even brief glimpses of their personalities. But with this demon she got...nothing.

She flexed her wrists as she stepped onto the same block as her visitor, making sure her daggers were easily accessible. Talia felt the weight of his gaze as she strode forwards. Did he know who she was, what she was, or was he merely hunting?

She stopped a few feet from the demon and crossed her arms.

"I would suggest you turn around and walk away before you give me a reason to kill you."

"Some would argue you already have several reasons," a

cultured voice replied.

A voice she knew too well.

Devlin stepped forwards into the pale glow of the street lamp.

He looked the same as he always had. Tall, dark and breathtakingly beautiful. The same stunning green eyes she remembered studied her in silence, drinking in the sight of her. He wore all black, as usual, and she knew if she checked, his suit and overcoat would have designer tags. He always had loved luxury and pleasure.

Talia stood strong before him, hiding her shock behind her cool business façade. She was proud of her response, especially considering the dream she'd had the night before. The last thing she wanted was for him to see how badly his appearance spooked her.

She'd always wondered what she would do when she saw him again. Would she go for his heart with a dagger or throw herself at his feet and beg him to kiss her again? But now fantasy had become reality and she was helpless to do anything but stand frozen before him.

"Hello, Tali," he said softly.

"Don't call me that," she snapped. "I'm not that child anymore."

Something flickered in his eyes. If she hadn't known him so well she would have sworn it was pain. But she did know him, and she knew he'd never cared about her in any way that mattered.

"What are you doing here, Devlin?" she asked harshly.

"You challenged me to come get you," he reminded her.

Talia snorted. "Like I thought you'd come. You have better things to do than chase after an inconsequential human."

A frown marred his beautiful face. "You are many things, Talia," he replied, "but inconsequential is not one of them."

She hid her shock at his words.

"I need to speak with you," he said abruptly. "Shall we retire to your apartment?"

"Like hell I am letting you near my home."

"This is not a matter to be discussed in the streets."

"Ever heard of a phone?" she snapped, unyielding.

Devlin shook his head in exasperation. "I'd forgotten how stubborn you are."

"Not stubborn," she corrected. "Cautious."

He glanced at her sharply. "You cannot think I am any threat to you."

"As I learned the hard way, I don't know anything about you at all."

He actually took a step towards her, anger burning in his eyes, before he stopped himself.

Talia was shocked at the display of emotion, however small. He prided himself on forever being in control.

"If I wanted to harm you," he said through gritted teeth, "I'd have had ample opportunity before now."

"You knew where I was?"

"I look after what is mine."

"I've never been yours," she snarled.

He opened his mouth to reply but thought twice. Instead, Devlin drew a deep breath before speaking in an even voice. "I wish to hire you, Talia. Surely you do not discuss business with a client in the streets."

"I have an office," she replied. "Make an appointment."

"You would refuse to see me."

"Damn straight."

"You do not want to refuse me this time."

"Give me one good reason why I would ever want to associate with you again," she demanded.

"Because I want to hire you to track the demon who murdered your family."

Talia jerked back in horror.

"Still want to discuss this in the street?"

Talia could hear the impatience in his tone. Without another word she opened the door to her building and motioned him inside. He followed her silently as they climbed the stairs. No way was she stepping into a small elevator with a demon.

"I was surprised you chose to live here," Devlin said as he stepped into her apartment. "You always had the same taste for luxury I did."

"Nothing about me is like you," she denied.

Devlin flinched slightly.

Talia shrugged out of her coat and tossed it over the back of the white sofa. She motioned to the kitchen table and grabbed her notebook before she dropped into a chair.

Graceful as always, Devlin slid into the seat across from her.

For a moment she couldn't believe this was real. Devlin was sitting in her kitchen, staring at her with his beautiful eyes. He was still the most stunning man she'd ever seen. Every cell in her body burned simply from being near him. But she knew all too well she walked a dangerous road. Devlin's appeal was a deadly trap. It sucked you in and left you broken and bleeding.

"Tell me about the demon," she said to turn her mind away from painful memories.

"His name is Saleel."

The monster of her childhood finally had a name.

"How powerful is he?"

"He is almost as old as I," Devlin replied, "and, very likely, almost as powerful."

Talia stared at him in shock. As news went, it rarely got worse. She was tough, but at the end of the day she was still mostly human. It was impossible for her to kill something as strong as Devlin. She might hate her demon lover but never, even in her wildest fantasies of revenge, had she deceived herself into thinking she had the slightest chance of physically harming him.

In one sentence he had forever destroyed her dreams of killing the man responsible for her shattered childhood.

"Why did you come?" she demanded painfully. "Is this merely some new torment to inflict on me?"

He sucked in a sharp breath. "I would never hurt you."

She laughed bitterly, knowing the words for the lies they were. "I can't kill something as powerful as you. Now I will never be able to avenge my family. It would have been far kinder to let me live in ignorance."

"You cannot fight him, it's true," Devlin said softly. "But I can."

Talia looked at him sharply. "What?"

"You can sense him. You can track him. When you find him, I will kill him."

A shock too deep to be hidden showed on her face. "Why?" she asked, for once the old anger gone from her voice. "If he is as strong as you say, it will be dangerous for you. He might even be able to kill you. No demon puts himself at risk in such a way. Why would you?"

A self-deprecating smile twisted his lips. "He hurt you," he answered simply. "That is reason enough."

It was too much. Before her sat the hero from her girlish dreams, not the monster she had hated all her adult life. She couldn't handle the dichotomy. Talia pushed herself out of the chair, needing to put some distance between them. She paced across the room until she was as far away from him as she could get. Was he telling the truth? Would he honestly risk his life to kill the man who had hurt her? Why?

Maybe it was restitution, she mused. But his actions didn't fit with her image of him as a selfish demon who took what he wanted without consideration for who he hurt. Why would he wound her so badly in the past only to show up now as her saviour?

She turned back to face him from across the room. "I don't understand why you would do this."

A short laugh escaped him, filled with a world of pain Talia couldn't understand. For a moment he didn't move. He closed his eyes and turned away from her.

Talia shifted uneasily as she watched him. They were playing a game she didn't know the rules to. Everything he did was the opposite of what she expected.

Finally Devlin opened his eyes and looked back to her. She drew in a sharp breath. Gone was his wounded look, his air of vulnerability. Instead, the Devlin who sat before her was the one from her memories, the demon who ruled his world with an iron fist. He never did anything free and there was no mercy in his soul. Devlin pushed back his chair abruptly before striding over to her.

"I see you cannot believe I'd help you merely because you asked. So let's try a different path. Make a deal with me," he demanded, his tone hard.

Her body shook. "Even a child knows not to make deals with demons."

"But you are no longer a child," he replied, his gaze moving heatedly over her body. "Offer me a deal to win your vengeance."

"What could I possibly offer you to make you risk your life?" she asked, honestly bewildered. She had nothing to tempt him with even if she was stupid enough to make a deal.

"Use your imagination," he murmured, his eyes burning with unfulfilled need.

She sucked in a sharp breath. He wanted her to bargain with her body? She told herself she was disgusted even as her traitorous heart raced at the idea of being in his bed again.

"I don't sell myself," she snapped angrily.

"Think of it in a different way," he replied, showing no mercy. "You need my strength. I need your passion. A mutually beneficial arrangement, is it not?" He took a step forwards, forcing her to back up until her body hit the wall behind her.

"Is it such a repulsive idea?" he asked her softly, his breath fanning her face. "You know you would enjoy it as much as I. This is the only deal I'll offer you, Talia. I shall kill your monster and in return you will be mine for one night. After that you may leave my world forever. I will never seek you out again."

"You'll release me?" she whispered. "No more henchmen demanding I return?"

"You'll be truly free," he agreed.

For a price.

She looked up into the green eyes she'd seen only in dreams for six long years. Even hating him as she did, his nearness stirred up all sorts of unwanted desires. She owed it to herself to at least be honest. It would be no hardship agreeing to be his for one last night. In fact, she probably would have made a deal just to have him in her bed again.

One night. All she would ever have from him was one more night. Was she strong enough to take what he offered? If she did, she would have to be very careful to leave her emotions at the door. She'd learned the hard way nothing but pain came from loving this demon. It was a mistake she would never make again.

But if it was only sex... She admitted her body still craved his touch, even after six years.

"Okay," she whispered before she could talk herself out of it. "I will accept your deal. Kill the demon who murdered my family and I will give you one night."

There was no triumph in his eyes as she'd expected. If anything he looked even more miserable.

"Deal," he agreed in an emotionless voice. "Seal it."

Already she felt his magic staining the air around them, waiting for the deal to be completed. To seal a deal with a demon there needed to be an exchange of body fluids. The most traditional way was mingling a few drops of blood. Of course, there were other ways.

"How?" she questioned, feeling her body tingle with anticipation.

"Given the nature of our bargain, I think you know," he replied.

Sealed with a kiss.

She wet her lips nervously. If she couldn't even kiss him, how was she going to sleep with him? *Grow up, Talia,* she commanded herself. *Get it over with.*

Her hands shook as she raised them to cup his face. His body was cooler than hers, a fact she'd forgotten. Against her will her traitorous fingers trailed over his smooth skin, marvelling at his presence before her once more.

His hands rose to settle on her hips and she felt his touch burn through her jeans. No matter what happened in her life, she knew she would never react to another man the way she did to this one.

Rising on her tiptoes, she pressed her lips to his. Her touch was hesitant even though she wished to be bold. Part of her couldn't believe he truly wanted her, even given the evidence to the contrary.

But her worries were groundless. Devlin tightened his hold on her, pulling her closer as he took control. He kissed her desperately, as if he were as starved for her touch as she was for his. His tongue traced her lips and she parted them obligingly. He invaded her mouth, consuming her, claiming her. She felt the magic around them shift and change. The deal was being sealed. And if she remembered correctly the last part of the process would be rather painful.

She gasped as unseen fire licked along her skin. Devlin swallowed her cry as the magic settled onto their flesh, burning into them with invisible chains. The terms of their deal sealed themselves into her skin, only to be erased when their bargain was completed... Or if Devlin chose to release her. But she knew there was no chance of that happening.

She stumbled out of his arms, waiting for the last tingle of magic to disappear.

"God, I forgot how much that hurt," she breathed.

"I am sorry," Devlin replied evenly.

Moving away from him and the memory of their kiss, she tried to regain her composure. Only Devlin had the power to rattle her this badly, but she'd be damned if she let him see what effect he had on her.

"I'll start hunting first thing tomorrow," she said, trying to focus on the job at hand. "Can you give me any locations he's been recently?"

"Yes, but you cannot hunt him alone."

She snorted. "Trust me. There are no other sensers who will want to help me with this one."

"That's not what I meant." He gripped her arm and turned her to him. "Saleel is more dangerous than any demon you've faced before, Talia. You need me with you at all times. Until our deal is completed I am not leaving your side."

Her eyes widened in horror. "No," she refused flatly.

"This isn't a choice. You want this guy? Fine, but you have to deal with the consequences. I can't claim my night if you're dead."

She flinched and told herself it was because she didn't like being cornered, not because of the reminder that all he wanted was her body when she had once been ready to give him her heart.

"You can't be with me all the time. You have a very busy life."

"Not for the next few days I don't," he replied. "I will be here day and night, Talia, until Saleel is dead."

"And if I don't like it?"

"Too bad. You've had six years of freedom. You owe me at least a few days of obedience."

She jerked her arm from his grasp. "I owe you nothing. I was in your debt once but as far as I'm concerned my bill has been paid in full." With her innocence.

He didn't challenge her words but merely repeated, "I am not leaving."

Talia grit her teeth, already sensing defeat. She didn't want him around, but it was true she wouldn't be safe once she started tracking Saleel. No matter how much she hated him, she had to admit Devlin wasn't wrong about the danger the demon posed.

"You're sleeping on the sofa," she said with ill grace.

He bowed in acquiescence.

She growled at him as she stalked to the hall closet and grabbed a sheet and blanket. Throwing them at him, she gave him a final glare before she strode to her bedroom. Talia couldn't help slamming the door behind her.

Chapter Four

It took her a few minutes to remember who was in her home when she woke the next morning. When she did, she buried her head in the pillow with a groan. Devlin was here. And as the last nail in her coffin, she'd promised to sleep with him. She shivered at the thought, but not in fear. It was an impossible situation. How was she supposed to work with him, live with him and keep her heart safe?

Sounds came from the kitchen, letting her know her troublesome guest was up. With a sigh, she rolled from the bed and walked groggily to her dresser. Time to start the day and see what new heartache it would bring.

When she entered the kitchen she saw the table set with scrambled eggs and French toast. Devlin had cooked for her? Devlin didn't cook. He hired people for that.

"Did you make this?" she asked in shock.

Devlin glanced at her from the stove, spatula in hand. "You forget to eat breakfast when you're working."

How did he know she forgot to eat? But she was much too proud to ask. "Still, you made this? As in, cracked eggs like a human? You can conjure food with your magic."

"You don't like me using magic for small things," he replied with his back to her. "You've told me a million times."

Why do you remember that?

She longed to ask. Instead she slid into her chair and

reached for the eggs.

As she ate she felt Devlin's gaze burning into her. He watched her like a hunter, and for the first time in many years she felt vulnerable. Dominant, arrogant, demon lord Devlin she could handle. Breakfast-making, wounded, sexy Devlin was another problem entirely.

"I want to get started right away," she told him, wiping her mouth on a napkin and deliberately refusing to thank him for the delicious meal. "Tell me the last place Saleel was."

"According to my sources he likes to spend his nights at a club called the Shadow Walk."

"Never heard of it."

"It's a demon club, Talia. They don't take too kindly to sensers going there."

"Oh." Talia mulled over the new information. "Well, we'll just have to be fast. You sneak me in, I try and get a sense of Saleel and we get out."

Devlin looked amused. "Every demon will know what you are. I could tell when you were an untrained child. In the past years your power has only grown."

"Fine, mister hot shot," she snapped. "You come up with a plan."

"Sensers are not welcome in demon clubs," Devlin replied, "but allowances are made for demons powerful enough to make trouble. The owners will take offense to you waltzing into their bar. They will look the other way if I bring my lover in for a drink."

Talia blushed, inwardly cringing. "Okay," she said, trying to brush away her discomfort. "We can make that work for us. I'll pretend to be your lover in the bar while we search for Saleel."

"You have to be convincing," Devlin said with humour in his eyes.

"Pretend to want you? I think I'm a good enough actress to

pull it off," she replied sweetly.

He narrowed his eyes.

"Shall we go now?"

Devlin glanced at the clock. "I don't know about you, but ten o'clock is a little early for me to start drinking."

She rolled her eyes. "The faster we get there the better I can sense his trail. You know time is a factor here."

"What clubs do you know that are open at ten in the morning?"

She paused. "When do they open?"

"Early evening at the least," Devlin replied. He leaned back in his chair with a satisfied smile. "How will we pass the time?"

"I'm not spending the day with you," Talia snapped. Rising, she grabbed her dishes and tossed them into the sink. When she stalked into the living room Devlin was hot on her heels.

"Why not? After all it's been six years," he said lightly. "We have lots to catch up on."

"Really? How's Merilyn?" Talia froze and bit her tongue. Merilyn had been his primary mistress when she'd lived at his mansion. Had Talia truly asked about her rival out loud? Embarrassment reddened her cheeks. Trying to salvage the situation, she said casually, "Never mind. I don't care. Tell me how you found out about Saleel."

Devlin was silent for a long moment but she refused to turn back to him.

"I don't know how Merilyn is. I haven't seen her in six years."

Talia twitched in surprise.

"I haven't taken any lovers in six years," Devlin finished softly.

Closing her eyes, she wished she could believe his words. But unfortunately for her, she knew lies when she heard them. Devlin was an innately sexual being. Most demons were. There was no way he could survive for six years without sex.

"You know I won't believe you," she said over her shoulder. "Why even bother with the lies?"

Again he laughed, but she heard the pain and self-mockery in the sound.

"Of course," he said tightly. "Sit, Talia, and I will tell you of Saleel."

Slowly, she sat across the room from him.

"I have been looking for Saleel since I first took you in," Devlin said. "I never heard any word about his whereabouts. Truly, I thought he was long dead until he resurfaced two nights ago."

"Has he killed anyone?"

"Not yet. My guess is he's come back for a reason." Devlin raised his stunning eyes to hers. "He means to finish what he started."

Talia felt as if the blood in her veins had turned to ice. "He wants to kill me."

"Yes," Devlin agreed quietly.

The demon of her childhood was stalking her, bent on finishing her off once and for all. Talia swallowed hard. "Good thing I have you around," she said, trying to appear unaffected.

His eyes widen in surprise at her cavalier pronouncement.

"We simply catch him before he gets to me. Right?"

Devlin nodded sharply.

"Good." She stood. "I have some research to do on another case. Call me when it's time to go to the club."

She left the room before he had a chance to call her back.

In her room, Talia leaned heavily against the door. She'd had demons gunning for her before. It wasn't anything new. But this wasn't any ordinary demon. When she closed her eyes she still heard the screams of her parents. Her childhood had been ripped away from her and tainted with evil. Saleel had a lot to answer for.

She sank to the ground, touching the rose on her neck out of habit. The familiar gesture calmed her slightly. She wasn't the same terrified child Saleel had come up against before. This time she was a woman trained to destroy demons. Plus she had Devlin in her corner. She may not truly understand why he was helping her, but she knew enough about Devlin to know he was a demon of his word. If he promised to keep her safe, he would.

For a price, her mind added.

Yes, for a price. He never did anything for free. Demons looked out for their own interests first. She knew that well enough. But if one night with an old lover freed her of the fear she lived with, she considered it a good bargain.

Pushing herself to her feet, Talia decided to make use of her time. She opened her weapons closet and pulled out a few daggers. A rusty senser was as good as dead. Might as well get some practise hours in while she waited for the sun to set.

When Devlin knocked on the door, she was ready. Talia sat on her bed, staring at the dark city beyond her window.

"It's almost time," Devlin said as he stepped into her room.

"I'm ready." She'd dressed in her customary black but chosen a daringly low-cut shirt to dress up her outfit. The long sleeves covered the daggers hidden in wrist sheaths, and with her short hair and low neckline the black rose on her throat stood out like a beacon. Her tight black jeans disappeared into knee-high boots, each equipped with a thin blade hidden in the lining. She looked dangerous. She looked like a demon's lover.

Devlin had dressed for the occasion as well. Gone were his habitual suits. In their place he wore a black silk T-shirt that reminded her painfully of the one he'd worn the night she'd slept with him. Black breeches encased his legs, laced up the

117

sides all the way from hip to hem. He looked scrumptiously sexy and a part of her hated him for it.

"You know the plan?" he asked, sitting next to her on the bed.

"As soon as we get to the club I need to pretend I'm infatuated with you," she recited. "You'll cover me while I search for any sign of Saleel."

"Do remember to be careful," he told her seriously. "This club will not be happy with your presence. I'd rather not have to fight every demon there to get you out again."

"I'll be a good girl," she taunted.

Devlin snorted. "You have no idea how to be a good girl."

She had years ago. But he was right—the innocent Talia had died her last night in the mansion. The woman who'd walked out of his house had been a different person entirely. Now being good was the last thing she wanted.

"Good girls don't kill demons," she agreed with a cold smile, "and I love my job."

He narrowed his eyes at her. "Why did you pick that particular line of work?"

She shrugged casually. "Needed to pay the bills."

"With the blood of my brethren?"

"Seemed poetic justice."

"Why?" he asked harshly.

Talia refused to look at him. No way was she letting him dredge up the painful past she was doing her best to forget. "We should go," she said, pushing off the bed. "The night is young and we have work to do."

Devlin sighed but let his questions drop. Resigned, he followed her from the room.

Talia stared up at the Shadow Walk's entrance with trepidation. Already she felt the presence of the demons within.

It battered at her like a storm. All her instincts were telling her to run, and yet she glided closer and closer to the club.

Devlin reached out and wrapped an arm around her waist, pulling her to his side. "Walk strong," he commanded her. "This is definitely a time when it's okay to look dangerous."

"Right," Talia breathed, straightening her shoulders. "I'm ready."

Together they strolled up to the bouncers. They took one look at Devlin and stepped aside. Both the demons at the door hissed softly as Talia walked by, but she did her best to ignore it.

The club was unlike anywhere she'd been before. They walked down a long staircase to the main floor and Talia realised it was all underground. She supposed it made sense since some demons had light sensitivity and others preferred to live completely underground.

Pounding music filled the air and red lights lit the crowded dance floor. This was definitely not a place for humans. Here the demons were not even attempting to blend in. Looking over the crowd, Talia saw horns and wings. Red eyes watched her with unnerving interest and several men licked their fangs as Devlin guided her over to the bar. Talia squared her shoulders and added a roll to her hips. If they wanted to play she'd make sure she came out on top. Devlin had told her to be dangerous. Talia let a cold smile curve her lips as she strode through the crowd. She could do dangerous.

The bartender slipped up to them the minute Devlin leaned on the counter. Talia was mildly surprised by the respect he commanded without even trying. She knew he was intimidating but in her eyes he was still the man who had rescued her on the most horrible night of her life.

"What will it be?" the bartender asked.

"Can I order you a drink, darling?" Devlin asked, running his hand down her back.

Remembering her role, Talia shook off her nerves and smiled sweetly up at him. "Whatever you're having, love," she replied, pressing herself closer to him.

"Our special is a true bloody mary tonight," the bartender said, looking at Talia with a hostile gaze.

Talia's eyes widened.

"I'll have a whiskey on the rocks," Devlin said easily, ignoring the man's hostility, "and a tequila sunrise for my date."

Tequila sunrises had been her favourite drink as a teenager. Talia glanced up at Devlin, surprised by his memory.

The bartender quickly prepared their drinks and handed them over. As Devlin paid, Talia cautiously sipped her drink.

"How is it?" Devlin asked.

"Excellent for a tequila sunrise without the tequila," she replied wryly. "My, he must have thought I was underage."

Devlin smiled slightly. "I told you this place wouldn't welcome you."

"Yeah, well I believe you."

"Come on," he caught her free hand. "Let's get a booth and you can start looking."

They threaded their way through the dance floor even though Talia saw no free booths. Given the hostile stares and hisses coming her way, she hoped they found something soon. She had never felt this exposed before. Of course, she'd never been in a room crowded with demons before. Even living with Devlin, she'd never seen this many demons in one place.

They walked over to the row of booths lining the wall and Devlin strode to the first one. A young couple sat in the red velvet seats, laughing and flirting. They looked up in surprise when Devlin stopped before them and Talia actually saw their faces pale.

"Please, sir, help yourself," the girl stammered, pushing at her date to get out of the booth.

Devlin watched with an amused smile as the couple fled, leaving the booth empty.

"What are you, the boogie man?" Talia asked, sliding into the seat.

"Close," he agreed, sitting beside her. "Remember your role, Tali. You need to be closer to me."

"Don't call me that," she replied automatically as she let him pull her to his side. "Judging by the reception you're getting, I think you owe me an explanation. How big a bad ass are you in this town?"

"You lived under my roof for five years," he replied. "Didn't you pay attention?"

"I only saw Devlin the friend. These people see Devlin the demon."

"Mmmm," he murmured, tilting her face up to his. "Does this mean I can scare you into following my orders now?"

She smirked at him. "What do you think?"

"I think," he said, tracing his thumb over her lower lip, "it takes beings far more horrifying than I to make you cower." He replaced his thumb with his lips, kissing her lightly. "I never wanted to scare you, Talia."

She relaxed into his embrace, touching the tip of her tongue teasingly to his lips. Taking her up on her offer, Devlin kissed her more forcefully. His hand trailed over her body, running up her abdomen to loosely cup her breast. She gasped into his mouth, nipping him lightly in warning. Even if it was a cover, she didn't do heavy petting in public. A girl had to have standards when sleeping with the damned.

"Your acting is very convincing," Devlin taunted quietly as he trailed his lips down her throat.

"I learned from the best," she snapped without thought.

Devlin jerked back, regarding her with puzzled eyes. Talia knew he was about to ask questions she didn't want to answer.

Victoria Davies

In order to distract him she rose up on her knees and swung a leg over his thighs. Straddling him, she cupped his beautiful face in her hands and kissed him passionately.

His hands gripped her hips to steady her as he thoroughly enjoyed her onslaught. When she finally drew back she was out of breath and more than a little turned on.

"As much as I am enjoying your...acting," Devlin said. "You should see if you can pick up anything on Saleel."

"Yeah," she agreed breathlessly, ignoring the hard bulge pressing between her thighs. "I'll try."

Devlin drew her closer to him, hiding her face in his chest. "Close your eyes," he whispered. "Cast out your senses. I've got you."

Relaxing into his hold, Talia did as he said.

"Quietly, Tali," she heard Devlin whisper in her ear.

She didn't have time to correct his use of the nickname. Knowing she'd been too obvious with her powers, she pulled back, softening her scan. She didn't want the other demons alerted to the fact that she was working tonight. They tolerated her for the moment. The last thing she wanted to do was start a bar fight in a demon club.

Devlin continued to trail kisses across her skin as she worked, moving her body to the pounding beat of the music. Talia forced herself to ignore how good it felt to be in his arms.

Concentrating hard, Talia worked her powers through every inch of the club, looking for any sense of the demon she sought. The search was frustratingly hard, especially since she couldn't use her full range of powers. Being subtle definitely sucked.

Then, without warning, she felt it. At the very edges of her senses she felt a sickeningly familiar tingle. It was one she had felt before, right before she dove from her bedroom window.

"Got him," she whispered, nauseated. "Backdoor."

"You're sure?" Devlin asked.

Talia pushed herself up and nodded. "He feels the same in my head," she confessed softly. "I can still remember what it was like to find him in my house..."

"Shhh," Devlin soothed, wrapping his arms around her. "He'll never touch you, Tali. I'll keep you safe."

For once, she didn't argue with him. Clutching her old protector to her, she tried to steady herself and push away the fear. She could fight this nightmare. She hadn't gotten her reputation by handing out flowers and hugs to the monsters she hunted. This was simply one more job. Besides, this time she had the ultimate ace in the hole. She might hate Devlin, but even she acknowledged he was a more vicious warrior than she'd ever be.

When she was in control once more, Devlin helped her to her feet and expertly navigated them through the crowd towards the backdoor.

"Which way did he go?" Devlin asked as they stood at the entrance.

Talia closed her eyes, touching the door handle lightly. "He went out," she said.

Without a word, Devlin opened the door and guided them up the cramped stairs. They exited into a dark, empty alley. Closing her eyes, Talia tried to pick up the trail. It was old and hard to find. Saleel had been trying to cover his tracks, which meant he knew what she was.

Sensing wasn't a science. She couldn't close her eyes and magically know what the demon she was chasing would do. It was more like she sensed the shadows people left behind. Everyone left traces of themselves as they went through their lives. Her job was to find those traces and immerse herself in them until she saw and felt everything the demons had. Sometimes it was easier than others. Saleel, unfortunately, was not such a case.

Opening her senses to the alley, she unleashed her full

powers. There had to be a hint of him somewhere.

She moved blindly around the alley. Sometimes she picked up stronger images if she stood in the same spot her marks had been in. If she was lucky enough to cross his path everything would be much easier.

Devlin stayed silent as she waltzed around the alley. This was her area of expertise, not his. Wisely, he knew enough to stay out of her way.

Stepping slowly through the space before her, Talia felt a sudden rush of excitement and stopped cold. The emotions swirling within her were definitely not her own. All she should be feeling right now was fear and disgust. Freezing in place, she forced herself to open up to Saleel's emotions. She needed to sense his desires, his plans. Though it went against every instinct in her, she welcomed in the feelings of her family's killer.

Chapter Five

He had stood here last night, right where she was. He'd looked up at the sky. Talia felt her head tilt back in grisly mimicry of her nightmare's movements. He'd breathed in, happy to be back in the city once again. Talia felt hungry and knew he'd been considering feeding. She blanched as she realised why he hadn't attacked some poor unsuspecting person. Anticipation was half his fun. He wanted to fantasise about her death instead of sating the need with some stranger. He was saving all his hunger for *her*.

Talia faltered, too horrified to look deeper. But this was the first step of the trail. She needed to know where he went next. She was a professional. This was her job. There was no room to be squeamish, not when the stakes were so high. Concentrating once more, she forced herself back into Saleel's emotions. He'd been happy when he walked out of the alley. Talia felt her feet moving of their own accord, following the killer's footsteps. He'd left the alley and turned right. One place in particular had been forefront in his mind.

"He went to my childhood house last night," Talia gasped, jerking from her trance. "Devlin, he went to my house."

The thought of Saleel in her home again turned her stomach. She thought she could be strong through this but she didn't know how to stand tall in the face of such horror.

Devlin put a hand on her shoulder but she shrugged it off.

Instead, she ran her fingers over her rose mark. *Courage,* she thought. *You can do this. You can survive this.*

"We should go," she said, straightening her shoulders. Her childhood home was the last place she wanted to go, but as usual she had no choice. Talia walked stiffly from the alley, a silent Devlin trailing behind her.

It was a short drive to her old home. When they arrived, Talia was surprised to see it was inhabited. Some other family lived in her house, no doubt clueless to its history of horror. Somehow she'd imagined it'd stood empty all these years.

"What did he do here?" Devlin asked.

With a sigh, Talia got out of the car. She walked to the front of the yard and closed her eyes.

It was easier this time to sense Saleel's presence. She knew immediately where he'd stood, moving automatically into the same spot at the head of the walkway. He'd stood here and watched the house. Talia swallowed hard as she realised he'd wondered if he should kill this family too. The hunger was there and the desire to destroy. He watched the family at dinner, saw the smiling children and loving couple and wanted to rip them apart.

Talia forced herself to go deeper. Why hadn't he killed these people? The answer slowly bubbled to the surface. He hadn't wanted to alert Talia to his presence. A mass murder in her childhood home would have been too much of a coincidence to ignore. His game with her had saved this family. At least it was one thing to be grateful for.

"Where did you go?" she whispered to herself, scanning harder. He'd watched the family for a long time, trying to decide whether or not to attack. When he was finished he'd gone to...the cemetery.

Talia got back into the car, choking back the bile in her throat. "He is going to my family's graves," she informed Devlin.

He hissed in anger.

"Saleel wants to admire his work." She shook her head in disgust.

Devlin shifted the car into gear and then headed for the cemetery. "We'll get him," he told her.

"Promise?"

"You have my word."

Talia smiled bitterly as she rubbed the rose on her neck. It was an absent movement born out of habit. She didn't even think about who she was doing it in front of.

Devlin watched her actions with hooded eyes. "Why do you do that?"

"Do what?"

"Touch the rose."

She dropped her hand as if it burned her. The rose and the events surrounding its appearance were topics she never wanted to speak of, but Devlin was waiting for an answer. Sighing, she replied, "I touch it for strength. It's a symbol of a horrible mistake in my life. Touching it reminds me to never let myself be that foolish again. I have to be strong."

"Horrible mistake?" Devlin bit out. "Nice to know."

"You asked," she snapped.

Devlin's eyes darkened in anger but he held his tongue. They drove the rest of the way in silence.

When they arrived at the graveyard Talia got out without a word and started down the familiar walk to her family's graves. She never spared a glance for Devlin.

They hiked through the dark cemetery and Talia tried her best not to be freaked out by the creepy setting. It was an old cemetery, the kind featured in horror films. It wouldn't be hard to imagine a monster lunging at them from behind an old grave. *Not a monster*, she amended grimly. *A demon.*

Finally, they crested the hill and saw her family's graves. She sucked in a sharp breath when she realised what awaited her.

Four white lilies lay before each headstone. Four dead white lilies.

"Monster," she whispered, too angry to feel anything.

Devlin held out a hand. Fire shot from his palm and burned all the offending flowers to dark ash. Talia shook with anger. How dare he come here to mock his victims? Did he have no decency at all?

"I want to kill him with my bare hands," she snarled.

Devlin laid calming hands on her shoulders. "I know but now is not the time to give in to your anger. We have to find him before we can slice him into tiny pieces."

Knowing he was right, Talia tried to shrug off the consuming rage gripping her. Even as she made the attempt she knew she wouldn't be able to shake this emotion. She couldn't sense others' feelings if she was all blocked up with her own.

"I can't," she cried, tears of frustration and rage pooling in her eyes.

"Talia," Devlin said, turning her around. "Look at me."

Reluctantly, she raised her eyes to his.

"I know this is impossible," he told her. "I wish I could do this for you. But I can't. You're the senser. We need your powers if we're going to stop this guy before he hurts anyone else. I know you can do this. Close your eyes. Take a deep breath. You have such strength in you," he murmured softly. "I always knew that. Do this for your family. Do this so you can feel safe again. Saleel robbed you of something infinitely precious. Help me make him pay."

Still shaking with anger, she tried to do what Devlin asked. She closed her eyes and focused on Devlin. Talia felt his hands on her, felt his nearness. She felt safe around him, even after the pain he'd put her through. Maybe she always would. After all, no matter what he'd done to her as an adult, he'd still saved her life as a child.

Concentrating on her lover helped her let go of some of the anger. Slowly, she became aware of Devlin's emotions. Using her powers, she tried to draw deeper. She sensed the turbulent emotions swirling through him. Lust was in the forefront but also anger at what Saleel had done to her. She saw his protective streak and smiled slightly. But there was more. She just couldn't see it all. Something important was missing. Something to do with her rose—

Devlin shook her roughly. "No, Talia!" he yelled at her.

Talia jerked back, blinking.

"I didn't give you permission to invade my feelings," he growled.

"Sorry. I was only trying to move past my anger. I did it without thinking."

He closed his eyes in frustration. "Try and sense Saleel," he told her, anger heating his voice. "And never turn your tricks on me again."

She swallowed, guilt clawing at her. She could have stopped much sooner had she wanted too. But the thing was she didn't want to. She wanted to know all his secrets. If she understood more about him, maybe he wouldn't be able to confuse her as much as he did.

"Sorry," she said again, turning back to the graves.

Anger washed over her once more, but this time she let it flow by her without engaging in it. She had no time to waste right now.

Closing her eyes, she opened her senses to Saleel.

Sickening waves of pleasure buffeted her. She tried to hold back her nausea as she felt his twisted pride when he looked at the destruction he caused. He'd been happy as he stood over the graves of her family. The idea that any creature would take

129

such delight in the wanton devastation he'd wreaked turned her stomach.

"Feel his plans," Devlin instructed, resting his hands on her shoulders. "Breathe past the emotions and see where he went next."

Talia did her best to hold on to Devlin's voice and use it as her anchor. He wasn't like the evil she was touching. Devlin may have hurt her emotionally but he would never harm her physically. He was her safe harbour, even now.

Sifting through the monster's emotions, she tried to catch traces of what he'd been planning as he stood here. Where was he going next?

The answer was elusive. She felt the presence of the thought she searched for but every time she tried to bring it into focus it disappeared like a dream.

"Dammit!" she cursed.

"Breathe," Devlin said, his voice calm. "Take it slow."

With careful precision, Talia tried again to catch the thought. She almost had it. Just a little more...

She gasped in horror, breaking her connection.

"Where did he go?" Devlin asked.

Talia gasped for breath, trying to calm her racing heart. "My apartment," she whispered finally. "Devlin, last night he headed for my apartment. If you hadn't been waiting for me..." The demon of her childhood would have ripped her apart and she wouldn't have been strong enough to stop him.

Talia was crushed in Devlin's embrace before she even felt him move. "Christ," he whispered in horror.

His arms were tight around her. Even though she drew comfort from his embrace, Talia knew she walked a slippery road. She had to put distance between them, even if she didn't want to. Especially if she didn't want to.

"Devlin, let go," she commanded, squirming in his arms.

"Please...give me a minute," he begged softly. "I almost lost you last night."

Instantly, she stilled. Fear flowed over her like an icy wave. She had almost met the same fate as her family and she hadn't known. She hadn't felt anything but the joy and pain of seeing Devlin. What if it had been Saleel who waited for her in the shadows? She'd be dead now and she hadn't even sensed he was there.

The scope of the demon's powers rocked her. If he had the ability to hide his presence it meant he was far stronger than she'd thought. Devlin could be in real danger fighting this man.

Unable to help herself, she wrapped her arms around her demon. He held her tightly and for once she wasn't complaining. For a long moment they stood in the cemetery, locked together unmoving. Finally, Devlin dropped his arms and stepped back.

"If he went to your house last night he would have seen me there. He knows we're together now," he said, not looking at her.

"And he knows what I can do which means he'd anticipate all the places we'd go today."

"He's not in the cemetery. I would have felt him."

"Which means—"

"He is probably waiting close to your apartment."

"There's an empty parking lot out back. Perfect place for an ambush."

Devlin smiled crookedly. "I thought this would take longer. Looks like everything will be over tonight."

Talia looked at her demon and for once didn't feel the usual hate. "Are you sure you want to do this?" she forced herself to ask. "He could kill you."

"If I walk away he *will* kill you."

"Yeah," she agreed with a shiver.

Devlin reached out and tucked a stray piece of hair behind her ear, a tender look on his face. "I'm having no second thoughts, Talia. Not about something this important."

Talia stared at her protector. Was she really important enough to him that he would risk his life? God, she desperately wanted to be. Her need caught her by surprise and she shook her head to clear it of the disturbing thought. Glancing back at the car, she tried to focus on the matter at hand. "If you're sure about this we should probably go."

"Yes."

"Do you need anything?"

Devlin grinned wickedly. "What do you think?"

Talia swallowed. She'd never seen him fight in full demon form but even his half-form was dangerous. He'd be fine. He had to be.

"Let's go," she said.

Chapter Six

They pulled into the parking lot slowly. Both of them scanned the area, looking for hiding demons.

"Where is he?" Talia asked.

"He's out there."

"Maybe he decided fighting you is suicide and he left."

"He's out there," Devlin repeated.

Talia breathed in shakily.

Glancing at her, Devlin reached over and took her hand. "Everything will be all right," he promised.

She looked at him across the darkened car. So many nights she'd dreamed of being free of him. For years the thought had kept her going. Her hate gave her power. But right now, looking at him, she couldn't imagine a world without him in it. The pain and betrayal he'd put her through years ago didn't seem to matter as much as it used to. The bottom line was she didn't want him hurt. She didn't want him taking any chances for her if it meant his death.

"I'm scared," she whispered.

"I know." His tone was heartbreakingly gentle.

"For you," she corrected him. She squeezed his hand. "Don't die," she commanded, not meeting his eyes.

Devlin sat in silence for a long moment, studying her bowed head. "Would that distress you?" he asked.

Talia swallowed hard before nodding once.

"Why?" he breathed.

Talia dropped his hand and looked out the window. "You saved me as a child," she said. "Of course I wouldn't want to repay you by getting you killed."

Devlin's bitter laugh cut her like a blade. "Of course," he agreed. "Well, my dear, do not worry on my account."

"Just be careful," she muttered.

"Always," he said shortly before swinging out of the car.

Talia squeezed her eyes closed for a second. Couldn't she have said something supportive or encouraging before sending him off to fight for her? What was wrong with her?

With a sigh, she opened the door and got out. Closing the car door, she scanned the parking lot. No matter how hard she tried, she couldn't feel Saleel anywhere.

"Look sharp," Devlin said as the shadows around the parking lot seemed to twist and grow until the darkness surrounded them, blocking out the street lights.

"Oh hell," Talia said, inching closer to Devlin. This demon controlled light? Definitely not good news.

"Stay by the car," Devlin told her, casting a last glance her way. When she nodded her agreement, Devlin rewarded her with a slight smile before he sauntered forwards.

"Greetings, Saleel," he called.

"Greetings, Devlin," a disembodied voice replied. "I have no fight with you. Step aside and give me the human."

"Sorry," Devlin shrugged. "She's mine."

"We do not court death so lightly." The demon sounded truly surprised.

"Nothing I do is ever done lightly," Devlin replied. "Will you withdraw?"

"I cannot. My failure to kill her has haunted me for years. Her death will be my solace."

The voice sounded calm as he talked about her impending death. Talia shivered in dread.

"It appears we are at an impasse," Devlin said. "Remember, Saleel, it was you who started this fight. We do not attack humans under other demons' protection."

"I found her first," the voice said. "If anything, I have the prior claim."

Without any warning, Devlin twirled around with a snarl, shooting a laser of light from his palm. The light hit the shadows and a dark figure leapt out of the way, rolling on the ground.

Talia gasped in surprise as the man who murdered her family rose to his feet and shook out his coat.

"How unsporting," he said.

He looked so...normal. Saleel was a tall man, loose brown hair curled around his face giving him an almost boyish charm. He smiled easily, and if Talia hadn't known who he was she would have thought him handsome. It made her sick. A man as evil as he was should look the part.

The demon strolled towards them. His black eyes flickered past Devlin and met hers.

"Hello, darling," he said with a twisted smile. "Have you missed me?"

Devlin moved to stand before Talia, using himself as her shield. "Don't talk to her."

Talia gripped Devlin's coat with shaking fingers. She remembered the way Saleel felt in her head. It was as if the night her family died were happening all over again.

"I'll do more than talk to her," Saleel replied with his boyish smile. "Once you are dead."

Devlin hissed, baring fangs that hadn't been in his mouth a moment ago.

"Come now, Devlin, such passion over a human? What if I promised to get you a new pet?"

"You won't live long enough to fulfill any promises."

Saleel hissed viciously, his charm dropping away. "Do not tangle with me," he warned.

"Get back, Talia," Devlin said, ripping off his coat and crouching defensively.

Talia stumbled back to the car, knowing she'd only be in Devlin's way if she tried to fight Saleel.

Devlin changed before her eyes. Razor-sharp claws elongated from his fingers, coupled with the killer fangs in his mouth. He grew taller, filling out with muscles her Devlin didn't normally have. Pointed ears peaked from his now-wild hair and black tattoos trailed over his skin in a language long dead. The green of his eyes bled pure black, no hint of white showing in his gaze. He looked feral and vicious. Even to Talia's eyes, he was completely terrifying.

She'd never seen this side of Devlin before. He'd been very careful to keep it from her. This form was one demons changed to when they needed every drop of their power. Usually Devlin was more than a match for his enemies in his human form. Judging from his complete change, Talia knew Saleel posed a real threat.

She turned her stunned gaze to their enemy and saw Saleel going through a similar transformation. Gone were all hints of the boyish, charming man. In his place there stood a monster ready to fight to the death.

Without warning, Saleel charged.

Talia held her breath as the demons clashed. Claws flashed before her eyes and terrifying snarls rent the air. They moved almost too fast for her eyes to follow.

Saleel slashed at Devlin with his vicious claws, trying to sink his fangs into his opponent's jugular. Talia cried a warning even as Devlin twisted out of the way, narrowly avoiding a death blow.

When flashes of fire lit the dark, Talia knew Devlin was attacking with magic as well as physical strength. It looked like her demon needed every advantage he had. Saleel must be stronger than he'd anticipated.

Talia watched in stunned silence as the two ancient, powerful beings tried to obliterate each other.

Grunts of pain filled the air and Talia smelled the tang of freshly spilt blood. Both demons had been wounded. Devlin attacked with blinding speed even as dark blood pumped sluggishly from his shoulder. Baring his teeth, he lunged at Saleel. He wrestled him to the ground before the other demon blasted him off with a burst of hot fire.

Devlin rolled out of the way, patting out the flames that clung to him. It'd take more than a little fire to take down such an old demon, but Talia still winced in sympathy.

The two demons circled each other, each looking for an opening. It was excruciating watching them fight and knowing she was useless to help.

Or was she?

Talia inched backwards until she was able to slip the car door open without alerting the demons to her plan. Slowly, she crouched and reached a single hand inside. When her questing fingers felt the cool leather of her bag she grabbed it and yanked it out.

Crouching behind the car to hide her actions, she carefully withdrew the black gun from her bag. It was her Plan B backup. Demons didn't die from regular bullets, but if the gun was loaded with silver ammo it would slow them down. Clicking off the safety, Talia slowly stood.

She knew she'd only get one chance at this. If she fired at Saleel and missed, the demon would come after her. Worse, if she fired and hit Devlin then they were both dead.

Sliding towards the warring demons, she kept the gun hidden behind her body. She didn't want Saleel alerted to what she was going to do before she did it.

The two demons were locked too tightly for her to get a clean shot. Talia had always been a dagger kind of girl. She knew how to fire a gun but it wasn't her area of expertise. This time, however, she had to be perfect.

One chance, she thought. *Make it count.*

The demons grappled before her. Devlin had Saleel pinned to the ground but once again the demon fought free of Devlin's attack, launching himself into the air.

Talia whipped her head back, trying to spot the dark demon against the black sky. As if by magic, Saleel was completely hidden from view.

Devlin paced the ground, staring intently at the sky.

How long can he stay up there? Talia wondered, pressing her back against the car for protection in case he came after her.

Suddenly Devlin shot his hand up towards the sky. Deadly energy erupted from his palm to rip through the night like lightning.

A painful cry sounded as the attack hit home.

Caught by the fiery magic, Saleel thundered back to the ground, slamming into the pavement with brutal force. Devlin was on him in an instant. Curling his sharp claws, he lunged for Saleel's vulnerable throat.

Even as his body twitched from the surge of electricity thrumming through him, Saleel had enough strength to roll free of Devlin's attack. Saleel twisted like a snake and drove his own claws deep into Devlin's uninjured shoulder.

Devlin's cry of pain echoed through the empty parking lot. Talia flinched in sympathy, knowing how much pain her demon must be in. He never admitted to discomfort. Only something extreme would get a rise out of him.

Saleel turned his claws viciously, cutting even deeper. Devlin was forced to push back in order to free himself, losing his advantage over his foe.

As Devlin limped back, Saleel pushed to his feet. He looked down at his weakened opponent, but instead of jumping back into the fray to press his advantage, he turned to look at Talia.

Talia retreated a step when jet black eyes locked on her. Opening her sensing powers automatically, she saw the way his thoughts turned.

If Saleel killed her quickly it would eliminate the need to fight. Surely Devlin wouldn't continue if she was dead. There would be no point and demons were nothing if not calculating. They did only what was to their best advantage. Saleel was banking on her death ending the battle. He could kill her and escape. There was no downside in his mind. Well, except for one.

Talia flinched as she read how Saleel wanted to prolong her death. The deranged demon wanted to truly enjoy it. Without Devlin, he would have made her scream for hours. But Saleel was a pragmatic demon. Pleasure was all well and good, but when the price was his personal safety, he was willing to forego his more sadistic desires.

He took a step towards her even as Talia raised her gun.

She pulled the trigger without hesitation. Demons moved too fast to chance having second thoughts. It was him or her, and she had zero qualms about killing when her life depended on it.

The first shot caught him in the heart but, with his changed demon form, she doubted the wound was more than a scratch. Demon skin was like armour when they converted fully.

Automatically, she adjusted her aim. The second bullet took him in the throat.

Saleel faltered but didn't stop.

Talia aimed for his forehead and fired. Again and again she pulled the trigger until she heard nothing but the useless clicks of an empty clip.

Her attack hadn't killed Saleel but to her surprise it had slowed him down. Dropping the gun, she drew both of the daggers sheathed on her wrists. If this was her end she'd go down fighting.

However, before Saleel reached her, Devlin rose from the darkness like an avenging angel.

Her bullets had slowed Saleel enough for the other demon to catch up. Devlin raced for Saleel and thrust his clawed hand into Saleel's back in a brutal assault.

Saleel froze, staring at her with surprise.

Talia was equally stunned, rising from her fighting stance. She watched a slow dribble of blood trail from Saleel's lips, staining his perfect, pale skin.

Before her, the demon of her nightmares choked on his own blood. Part of her was horrified by what she saw. Bullets hadn't pierced his flesh, yet Devlin was strong enough to drive his hand through the armour-hard skin? She shivered. Devlin had powers she hadn't even guessed at.

"Do you know what I'm holding?" Devlin voice split the stillness. The sound that emerged from his lips was rough and guttural, far from his own voice.

"Yes," Saleel choked out the word.

"Good."

Devlin jerked his hand out of Saleel and the demon dropped to the ground like a puppet whose strings had been cut. In Devlin's bloody hand, Talia saw Saleel's still heart.

Devlin squeezed the organ until it exploded in his hand, his face expressionless. He shook the mess to the ground and stepped back from his kill.

Slowly, he raised his gaze to Talia's.

She looked at him without any mask, unable to hide her feelings. In truth, she didn't know what she felt. For a long moment she could only stare at him until her gaze dropped to Saleel's lifeless body.

Devlin had frightened her with his strength and brutality, it was true. But more importantly, he had killed her monster. He'd fought a deadly battle for her and won. Devlin might be terrifying but nothing changed the fact that he was still her hero.

She took a stumbling step forwards, then another, until she stood before him. Before he could speak, she carefully wrapped her arms around him.

Devlin stood frozen in her embrace, as if he were unsure whether his touch would be welcome.

Stepping back from his stiff body, Talia looked up to meet his eyes. She showed him without words that nothing he did would ever turn her away. Especially not when his actions saved her life and endangered his own.

Devlin smiled slightly, his demon-black eyes bleeding back to his natural green. He looked past her and snapped his fingers. Blue flame leaped around Saleel's body, destroying all evidence of their fight.

Talia shielded her eyes from the brilliant glow of the unnatural flames. Instead of being frightened by the display of magic, she felt refreshed. The flames were cleansing the evil from her life. They took Saleel's stench and banished it forever from the world.

She looked back up at her demon as the flames started to dim.

He was watching her, not the fire. Devlin's eyes glowed as he lightly touched her face, tilting her chin up.

"I held up my side of the bargain," he told her softly.

She sucked in a sharp breath.

Now it was time for her to hold up hers.

Chapter Seven

Talia waited nervously in her living room, listening to the sounds of the shower running in the bathroom. Devlin was in there washing off the evidence of his battle and healing his wounds. When he was finished...

She jumped off the couch and began to pace around the room. When he was finished he'd come back into this room and expect her to fall into bed with him.

And what troubled her most was how little she was opposed to the idea.

She stalked into the kitchen and poured herself a glass of wine for courage. She'd watched Devlin kill a man. The battle had been vicious, leaving the air littered with magic and the ground drenched in blood. It was wrong to be thinking about sex right now. It was sick and twisted and completely unnatural. And yet she was.

For the first time since she was fourteen, she felt free. In the back of her mind she'd always known Saleel was out there somewhere and one day he might come back to finish what he'd started. Even as she tried to create a new life for herself, she'd been haunted by the ghosts of her past. But now she was safe. She was truly free from Saleel's nightmare, and her knight stood in the shower, waiting for his reward. Gratitude was too weak a word to cover what she felt for Devlin. So was lust.

She knew the right word to use but couldn't bear to even

think it.

Instead she focused on the present, on what she had gained. She was a free woman for the first time in her adult life, not hounded by fear or rage. She wanted the first act she committed as her new self to be making love to the one who meant everything to her, even if he was a demon.

Being with him wasn't about their bargain, if it ever had been. Talia smiled cynically. She had waited six years to be back in his arms. Even knowing she'd disappointed him their first time, she couldn't deny he was the best lover she would ever have. He'd bargained for one night and she was determined to make it one she'd cherish forever.

The bathroom door opened.

Heart pounding, Talia slipped back into the living room and waited. Within seconds Devlin stood before her. His hair was still slightly damp and his clothes stuck to the residual moisture on his body. He looked breathtakingly perfect. And for tonight he was hers.

Eagerly she stepped forwards.

"You kept your end of the bargain," she said huskily.

Devlin lowered his head. She felt his breath fan her face and held still in anticipation. She waited breathlessly for his kiss, but at the last moment he stopped.

"Christ," he swore softly, spinning away from her.

Talia flinched at the rejection. Was he remembering the last time they'd been together? Had it truly been that bad for him?

"I can't do this," he said, dragging a hand through his hair.

She struggled to keep her pain from showing on her face. What had she expected? After six years he'd magically decide she was the only one for him? Straightening her shoulders, Talia swore he'd never know how he'd managed to shred her again. It was her own fault for giving him the opportunity.

Devlin turned to look back at her and Talia made sure her

face was emotionless.

"I can't force you to do this," he told her softly. "Especially not after what you've been through tonight." He laughed hollowly. "Looks like I can't be the monster you thought."

"What?" Talia frowned in confusion.

"I release you," Devlin said in a voice filled with dark power.

Talia shuddered as the hidden writing lifted to the top of her skin and slowly floated from her arms. She felt the magic draining from her body. Nothing would force her to fulfill her bargain now. Her demon had let her go.

"Why did you do that?" she demanded, staring at her now bare arms.

A heartbreaking look crossed Devlin's face. "I know you hate me, Tali," he told her quietly. "But I was never capable of hurting you. Your nightmare is over now. You can go on with your life and forget all about me."

Impossible.

"Are you..." Her words trailed off as she wondered how to phrase her question and what she'd do if he gave her the wrong answer. Summoning her courage, she tried again. "Are you releasing me because you don't want to coerce me into doing something against my will? Or are you releasing me because you've decided you don't want me in your bed tonight?"

He looked at her as if she'd gone mad. "I've wanted you every night since you left," he said harshly.

Lies, she thought, but it still felt good to hear. "Then why push me away when you finally have me?"

He took a step towards her. Talia held her breath as he returned to her and tilted her chin up to see her face. "Do you want me, Talia?" he asked.

"Always." The word slipped from her lips before she could stop it. It revealed too much.

"There's no bargain," he said, wrapping an arm around her

waist. "I will not stop you from walking away."

"Stop trying to push me away if you don't want me to go," she said softly. "A girl's pride can only stand so much."

A devilish grin twisted his lips. "Forgive me, my lady," he murmured, "for my exceedingly foolish words."

"Make it up to me," she breathed.

"Oh, darling, I'll make it up to you all night long."

Fine by me, she thought dizzily as he claimed her mouth with his. There was nothing tentative about his kiss. He meant to claim her tonight and she had no protests. His lips slanted over hers, teasing breathless moans from her. Her knees buckled and she stumbled against him. All it took was one kiss from him and her body stopped obeying her commands. If he kept this up she wouldn't be standing very much longer.

As if reading her thoughts, Devlin swung her into his arms and charged through the apartment to her bedroom. He crashed through the door and staggered to the bed, dropping them both onto the large mattress without taking his mouth from hers.

Talia wrapped her legs around his waist as his mouth trailed down her throat. She tilted her head back, giving him better access. His lips touched the black rose and she felt a moment's hesitation. *It won't be like last time*, she swore to herself. She wasn't a fumbling girl anymore. She'd bring him to his knees if it was the last thing she did. No old scars would stop her now that they were finally together. She only had one chance to show him she was more woman than he could ever dream of handling.

"Do all demons move so slowly when it counts?" she taunted, trying to sound aloof.

"Slow, eh?" Sitting up, he gripped her shirt and ripped it off her.

"I liked that top," she complained, not mourning its loss at all.

"Oops," he replied, unapologetic. He ran light fingers across her abdomen, sending sparks of pleasure shooting through her. She shivered as he trailed his fingertips along the edge of her bra.

"This needs to go," he murmured.

"No arguments," she agreed, trying to catch her breath. She watched as one of his nails elongated into a demon claw. Hooking the claw around the front clasp, he sliced through the black material as if it were butter.

He pulled the offending lingerie from her body and stared down at what he'd revealed. The hot, hungry look in his eyes made Talia feel more beautiful than she ever had before. Enjoying his stare, she made no move to cover herself from his intense gaze.

Leaning down to nuzzle one breast, he said hotly against her skin, "You're heaven, darling."

"Says the demon," she said with a laugh. "What would you know of it?"

"I know of heaven," he whispered, looking up at her. "Heaven is when you're by my side. And true hell is when you're not."

How she wished his words were true and not perfect pillow talk. Banishing the unwelcome thought, she reached for her lover.

"I don't have claws to rip off your shirt, but if you don't move faster I'll try anyways."

Devlin pulled his T-shirt off without another word.

Sucking in a sharp breath, Talia stared at the spectacularly perfect male chest before her. How had she not remembered *that*? Something was wrong with her, that's how.

"See something you like?" he asked, smug.

In reply, she sat up and molded her mouth to his chest,

running her tongue around a nipple.

Devlin hissed in pleasure, one hand burying itself in her hair to hold her to him. She trailed her lips over the vast expanse of bronzed skin as her nails skimmed lightly up his sides. Talia revelled in the shuddering breath she felt him take. Dammit, she was going to make sure he never forgot her.

Pushing him down onto the bed, she trailed her lips lower until she felt the rough fabric of his pants against her face. She ran her tongue along the line of skin next to the material. Looking up his chest, she met his eyes as she pressed a kiss right over the top buttons of his fly. His green eyes glowed in the dim light and she felt a feminine thrill. Demon eyes stared down at her. Apparently she was doing something he liked.

Talia ran her hands up his powerful legs. When she reached his fly, she trailed her fingers teasingly over the clasp.

"Tali, *please*," he begged.

She undid the buttons with a flick of her fingers and lowered the zipper. Devlin uttered a low moan of pleasure as he sprang free from the constricting material.

"My, my," Talia whispered, staring at the large erection before her.

He watched her with wordless pleading in his eyes as she sat up slightly and ran a single finger along his length.

"Christ," he cried, arching off the bed.

A slow smile of satisfaction curved her lips. She did have the power to bring this invincible warrior to his knees.

"Did you say something?" she teased. Talia continued to trail her finger over him in the lightest of touches. Caresses meant to burn and torment, never to ease.

"Talia, touch me more strongly or crawl back up here and let me take over."

"Nah-uh," she denied. "This is my turn to play."

Good to her word, she lowered her head and ran the tip of

her tongue over the skin her fingers had teased only seconds before.

"Talia!" he shuddered.

She trailed her lips up his long length. By the time her mouth touched the tip of him she knew she had the power to drive him wild. Talia smiled with satisfaction when she saw his clawed hands fist the sheets. This was what she wanted, Devlin at her mercy. Parting her lips, she took him into her mouth, giving him exactly what he craved.

A wordless shout shook the walls. Talia practically purred in satisfaction as she worked her hot mouth over him. He twisted beneath her and she gripped his thighs to keep him still. She knew a man like Devlin hated to lose control, even in the most pleasurable of circumstances. The thought only made her hotter. How far could she push him before he broke down and begged her for the shattering release only she could give him? Talia trailed her tongue up his hard shaft, liking the thought.

His incoherent moans filled the air, urging her on. One hand reached down to tangle in her hair. She revelled in the desperate touch, wanting him wild and aching. Beneath her hands, she felt the tension in his body and knew he was straining for release. Should she be kind? Or should she tease him just a little bit more?

A wicked smile curved her lips. It was an easy choice. Talia drew him deep into her mouth one last time and sat back.

"*No!*" he cried. "Christ, Tali, you will destroy me."

"Good," she said, her voice unintentionally serious. "Let me destroy you." *The way you once did me.* She shook her head to clear it of the malicious thought.

Devlin reached down to grip her arms before pulling her up to him. Talia gifted him with a wicked smile as she slid up his chest. Her own body thrummed in anticipation. She wanted to feel his hands, or better yet his mouth, running all over her.

Nothing in her life had felt as good as being in his arms.

Kicking off his pants, Devlin pulled the waistband of her jeans and moved to rip them off her as he'd done her shirt.

"Uh-uh," she said, stopping him. "You have no idea how long it takes women to find jeans that fit."

"You have ten seconds to remove them," he growled.

It took her three.

Devlin rolled her under him. He pushed himself up on one elbow, gazing at her with a look of supreme dominance.

"You almost brought me to my knees," he whispered against her mouth. "My turn to play."

"Be my guest," she replied, gripping the sheets when he latched onto her breast.

Devlin flicked her nipple with his tongue. He trailed his fingers down her smooth skin until they were buried in the dark curls between her thighs.

She cried out as he slipped one finger into her hot passage.

"Dev," she gasped, rocking against his hand. Slowly, he moved in her, making her writhe with every stroke. When he slipped another finger into her she practically levitated from the bed.

"So tight," he whispered against her breast.

Because I've only ever been with you, she longed to say. "Doesn't matter," she gasped instead. "Hurry up."

He removed his fingers from her and Talia was unable to stop her cry of protest.

"Shhh," he soothed, raising himself up to press against her entrance.

Talia took a breath and looked up into his glowing eyes. She may have been ready for him, but Devlin was big enough that nothing about him was easy. Gripping his shoulders, she tried to relax and welcome him into her body.

She closed her eyes as inch by delicious inch he forced his hard shaft into her, stretching her to accommodate his foreign size. He held still when he was fully seated inside, giving her body time to grow used to his. She was touched by his gentleness when she knew by his eyes exactly how wild he must feel. She rolled her hips to reward him, letting him know she was ready for anything he had to offer.

His eyes burning into hers, he withdrew to the tip and surged back into her.

Talia arched off the bed, gasping in intense pleasure. If this was how he normally made love there was no way she'd survive the night.

Gripping her hips, he rocked into her at a demanding pace. He pulled her body up with his, moving her in time to his thrusts. Talia was only too happy to follow his lead, raising her hips to meet him every time.

She pulled his head down to kiss him passionately, her tongue mimicking the thrusts of his body. He pressed into her until both their bodies were slick with glistening sweat. Talia pumped her hips with desperate need. She felt the pressure within her building and had no thought other than finding total and absolute release.

Devlin turned more savage, thrusting into her without mercy or restraint. Talia was never one to complain about a good thing. She locked her legs around his waist, pulling him deeper.

"Devlin," she cried, feeling an earth-shattering orgasm creep tantalisingly close.

"Come with me, love," he commanded, shuddering above her.

Talia opened her mouth to scream as a pleasure unlike anything she'd felt before crashed over her. It drowned her in its blinding waves. She felt Devlin stiffen above her, shouting his own release. Every inch of her body felt as if it were exploding in pleasure. She couldn't move, couldn't speak, couldn't do anything but ride the inconceivable pleasure and pray it never ended.

Chapter Eight

Talia never wanted to move again. She lay tangled in the silk sheets, unable to do anything about the silly smile on her lips. True to his word, Devlin hadn't let her get any sleep the night before. After their first shattering orgasm they'd made love countless times. Talia lost track of the ways he'd taken her. He'd been hard and rough when she needed it and tender when her body had demanded something slower. Every movement had been perfectly attuned to her needs. It was as if he'd known her body even better than she did.

Looking around her room, Talia pressed her hands against her burning cheeks as she remembered their sexcapades. They'd made love in the bed, against the wall, before the mirror...

She buried her head in the pillows. How was she going to let him go?

The chilling thought dampened her pleasure. He'd bargained for one night and received payment in full. There was no reason for him to stay with her any longer.

Talia's heart clenched at the thought. He'd told her after their one night he'd never contact her again. She was free of him.

Just when she realised that was the last thing she ever wanted to be.

Victoria Davies

What a mess, she thought, closing her eyes tightly. What was she going to do? Beg him to stay with her a little longer or keep the tattered remains of her pride and watch him walk out of her life forever? Neither option appealed to her.

Carefully, she rolled over to see her lover's sleeping face. Would he want more? The old hurts crept up on her once more. When had she let him become so important to her again? She'd more than learned her lesson. But looking at his beautiful face, she knew the truth she could never voice. She'd never stopped loving him. Even if he left her forever it wouldn't change what she felt. Hell, she was a glutton for punishment.

As if sensing her distress, Devlin rolled towards her, his eyes opening. He smiled sleepily at her and she sucked in her breath at the sexy sight. It was one she wanted to see every morning.

"Good morning," he murmured.

"Morning," she chirped back.

He reached out to touch her cheek. "Thank you."

"Any time," she said and winced. That hadn't been what she'd meant to say.

A slight smile touched his lips, but already the sleep was fading from his eyes, leaving them painfully serious.

Talia rested on her elbows, looking down at him. She stared at his collarbone instead of meeting his questioning gaze. She wanted him befuddled by pleasure and wild with need. Not logical and intelligent. He could do too much damage in that state.

He trailed his fingertips over her bare skin, watching her watch him.

"We should get dressed," she said finally. "We've slept most of the day away."

"Why did you leave?" Devlin asked softly.

154

Talia tensed, drawing away from him. "Don't ask," she said harshly. "Don't ruin last night."

"I have to," he replied stubbornly.

She cringed as she saw his resolve, knowing he wouldn't be easy to put off this time.

"I have been asking myself that question every day for the past six years. I need an answer, Tali. I need to understand what went wrong."

With a sigh, Talia sat up, pulling the sheet up around herself. "Can't we forget the past? Maybe we could...start over." She made the offer tentatively. She didn't want to lose him, even if it meant giving up her pride.

"To start fresh I need to understand why we crashed and burned the first time. I need to know what to avoid."

She laughed harshly. "It's not you who needs to avoid anything. It's me. I'll do better this time."

"What do you mean?" he demanded.

Talia looked away from his too-perceptive gaze. "I won't make the mistakes I made the first time. Promise."

"What mistakes?"

Am I really going to do this? she wondered, panicked. Was she going to bare her heart to him and explain why she'd run the first time? He had a valid point. They needed everything in the open if they had any chance of navigating the turbulent waters of their relationship. And she wanted to. This time she was older and wiser. She wanted to fight for him instead of running the way she had when she was younger.

"All right," she capitulated. "Fine. Let's do this. I promise this time round I won't be as foolish as I once was. I won't look for more to our relationship than there is. I'll accept what we have and enjoy it while it lasts."

"What do you mean, more than there is?" he asked carefully.

She kept her gaze firmly on her painted red toenails. "I won't hope for you to love me the way I did when I was younger. Maybe I was rash to act the way I did," she acknowledged for the first time. "But when I woke up that morning and went to get a change of clothes your women were waiting for me. They had the decency to explain what the rose on my neck meant, and after learning I was such a thorough disappointment to you I couldn't bear to stay. The pride of the young and stupid."

Unable to stay beside him any longer, Talia threw herself from the bed, dragging the sheet with her. "I'm taking a shower," she said, her back to him.

"Wait." It was only one word but Talia felt the dark rage in it.

Stunned, she turned around to see Devlin in all his demonic glory. Very rarely had she seen this side of Devlin and now he'd changed twice in one night. His other self only showed through in the face of a rage so consuming he lost all control.

Slowly, she backed away, treating him the way she would a wild animal.

"I said wait," he snarled, watching her with black eyes.

She froze.

"What did the women tell you?"

"What?" She frowned. Of all the things to be angry at, she hadn't expected it to be her words about her rivals.

"Tell me exactly what they said."

Talia swallowed, recalling what had happened six years ago. "Merilyn pulled me into her room where the others were waiting. You had quite the harem." She couldn't keep the bitterness from her voice. "They tried to welcome me into their ranks. They gave me tips on how to hold your interest and told me I could expect to be invited to your bed once every ten days or so until you grew bored with me." She hadn't meant to say that. Her bitterness and hurt were too obvious. Conjuring the memory had torn her heart again, ripping into the wound she'd thought long since healed. Talia drew a shuddering breath, trying to get it together. She had to deal with this logically, be detached. Just pretend it was someone else's humiliation.

"They were playing with my hair when they saw the rose," she said in a cool voice. "The room was silent until Merilyn was finally kind enough to tell me what it meant."

"What did she say?" he demanded darkly.

Talia didn't want to remember this part. It had hurt unlike anything she'd ever experienced before or since. "She told me," she said, trying desperately to remain aloof, "the mark was a sign you'd fed on me, which I acknowledged. Those women looked at me as if I were the most pitiable creature they'd ever seen. I noticed no one else had the same mark and I asked why. Merilyn told me you'd never fed on them. They weren't your meals." Talia cringed as she said the hated word. "She told me you only needed to feed on blood when the..." She laughed bitterly, revisiting the painful memories of her younger self. "When the sex was so unsatisfying you had to sate yourself with food instead. The fact that no other woman in that room had the mark meant I was the only one clumsy enough in bed to reduce you to feeding."

"Finish it," Devlin said harshly when she stopped talking.

Finally, she looked back at him, knowing she couldn't hide the heartbreak in her eyes. "Being with you was the best night of my life," she said, not caring how trite it sounded. "And to learn you valued me about as much as you did a cheeseburger broke my heart. I knew I wasn't the type of woman you usually liked, but I thought you'd be a little patient with me. Teach me what I didn't know. To be written off so fast by the man who was my whole world..." She cleared her throat, touching the rose out of habit for strength. "I decided I would not let you cast me out. I would go of my own will. I packed my bags and left before I could humiliate myself any further in your eyes."

She looked anywhere but at him, aware that she had finally done the very thing she'd left to avoid.

"I really need that shower," she whispered, turning.

Devlin bounded from the bed, ignoring the fact he was naked, and grabbed her arm. He spun her around to face him.

"I never fed from those women because I never lost my control so completely the way I did with you. I couldn't hold anything back when I was in your arms. You reduced me to my absolute weakest and loved me anyways."

Talia blinked in surprise. She looked up at him hesitantly, feeling as if one wrong word would shatter her.

"And even if I had fed from one of them out of boredom, they would not wear the rose," he told her.

"Why?"

"Because that mark is reserved solely for my wife."

Talia jerked back hard enough to hit the wall with a solid bang.

"The night we met," he told her quietly, "I woke knowing someone important to me was in danger. I rushed into the night, following the faint screams in my mind for help. It was you, Talia, reaching out to your mate. I understood what was happening as I searched for you. After all my years of being alone, I'd finally found the woman destined solely for me. But when I entered the alley all I saw was a frightened little girl."

He snorted in black amusement. "You can imagine my horror when I realised the woman I'd been waiting centuries for was not a woman at all. She was a child and she was terrified of my race. But nothing changed the fact that I needed to protect you. I did the only thing I could. I took you with me and waited five painful years for you to grow up."

"That can't be true," she breathed. "You never even looked at me lustfully until I asked you to."

"The day of your nineteenth birthday I told Merilyn and the

others I would never touch them again," he said, denying her words. "I gave them a week to vacate the mansion. You were old enough to take your place by my side and I was determined to seduce you there. There would be no other woman for me but you. Then you wished for me on your birthday." His soft smile was heartbreaking. "I told you, Talia, to be careful of your wish. It was impossible to let you go after hearing those words."

"But the women said—"

"I had discarded them for a naïve, innocent girl. They lied to you for revenge. My night with you was absolutely perfect, Tali. There was nothing dissatisfying about you. I slept so long the next day because you completely exhausted me." He smiled wryly. "But when I woke I discovered the woman I loved more than life had fled from me. Merilyn told me she found you in tears. She said you'd been terrified by me and feared returning to my bed. She told me to give you space, you'd come back when you were ready."

"So all this time..."

"I thought my mate feared my touch," he said, finishing her thought. "I thought I'd... hurt you in some terrible way. And as the years passed my fears only grew. I had no idea how to make it up to you."

"Hurt me?" She snorted. "What we just did should prove I've never feared you that way. Hell, losing your virginity is supposed to suck and instead it was the most mind-blowing experience of my life. Well," she amended, "it was up until last night anyways."

He pulled her roughly into his arms. "You never feared me," he breathed like a prayer.

"And you never used me." She still couldn't believe it. "Dev, so many years."

He closed his eyes in pain. "If I had come after you, tried to talk to you, we could have cleared up all these misunderstandings. We could have been together."

"Damn pride," she agreed. "Being mortal around you will suck enough without wasting six of my good years."

Devlin eased her back slightly. "Tali, when demons mate it's not for a smattering of years. It's forever."

"But I'm not immortal."

He bent down and trailed his lips over the rose. "You could be. I started our union six years ago. All you have to do is complete the ritual and our life forces will be bound together. You will live as long as I do."

She sucked in a sharp breath. "What do I have to do?"

"Do you remember how I gave you the rose?"

"You bit me while we were...in the throes, so to speak."

"Exactly. You have to do the same. Our mingled blood seals the contract. The same mark will appear on my throat. Once bound, it is unbreakable."

"Demon magic," she breathed.

He nodded sharply.

She looked up at him, considering what he'd told her seriously. Was she ready for forever with this man? Reaching up, she traced her fingers over his face. Who was she kidding? She'd been ready since she was fourteen. She'd spent six years trying to hate him and failed miserably. Her life was incomplete without him by her side. In a choice between a single lifetime and an eternity with his love, she knew what she'd pick.

"Well," she said, rising to her tiptoes to kiss his lips. "If we need to be in the throes maybe we should move back to the bed."

A fierce joy more powerful than anything she'd ever seen washed over his face.

"I love you," he told her before he kissed her with burning passion.

"God, me too," she said when she was able. She smiled up at him. "I'll make you a new bargain, demon. I'll give you the rose if you'll promise to love only me for eternity."

Devlin grinned as he waltzed her backwards towards the bed.

"Deal."

About the Author

To learn more about Victoria Davies please visit www.victoriadavies.ca. Send an email to Victoria at contact@victoriadavies.ca or join her on Facebook at www.facebook.com/victoria.davies.

My Avenging Angel

Madelyn Ford

Dedication

To Rich, thanks for putting up with this writing thing. I love you. And to my kids, for thinking macaroni and cheese is the best dinner ever. And a special thanks to Kristin, for having to read this story "just one more time". You're the best.

Prologue

Asmodeus stared down at the sniveling, postulating human, a sneer lifting the corner of his lips. He'd been ripped from his dimension, brought to this godforsaken plain known as Earth and he wasn't happy about it. In fact, if it hadn't been for the protection spell the man had woven into the circle surrounding him, Asmodeus would have killed the weakling for his audacity.

"Why have you summoned me, human?" he demanded, taking a step forward to test the barrier. He was delighted to find a slight weakness in his invisible cage. He could work with that.

"I ask your help, my lord," came the timid reply.

Folding his arms across his wide chest, Asmodeus watched as the man remained on his knees, head bowed to his chin, and found the action mildly mollifying. He might just hear the human out before he killed him.

"You called me forth to ask my help?"

"Yes." Brown eyes met his briefly before dropping back to the floor. "There is a woman—"

"I am the Lord of Wrath, king of the vengeance demons, not a damn matchmaker. Release me now, human," he growled, rethinking his earlier plan. He was going to enjoy taking this creature apart piece by tiny piece.

The man's head shot up, surprise lining his features. "I

don't want her love, my lord."

"No? Then what is it you seek?"

Eyes narrowing, a look of intense hatred bleeding into those brown orbs, the man growled, "I want the bitch dead."

"And if I do this for you? What are you willing to sacrifice?"

"Anything. Everything."

Asmodeus studied the pitiful being for a moment, then a grin slowly spread across his face. Dead he could do. In fact, he would relish every moment of the act: skin tearing beneath his nails, blood oozing forth and the fragrant cries of pain tickling his ears. But he was getting ahead of himself. First there was payment. And then he had to decide if he would kill the human after reaping his soul or just maim him, leaving him alive to do Asmodeus's future bidding. Oh, so much pain, so little time.

With one tiny hand, she brushed sweat-drenched hair from her eyes while she reached out with the other, fingers trembling slightly, to nudge the prone figure on the bed.

"Mommy," she whispered. Her gaze fell to the empty bottles littering the bedside table and she knew it was a waste of her time. Mommy always got like this after the bad man left. But she had to try. "Please, Mommy. You need to wake up." She grew louder as her urgency rose. "The bad man is coming back. We have to hide."

The soft voice in her ear told Tory she was running out of time. Hands swirled out of the mist in an attempt to herd her away from Mommy but she clutched Mommy's shirt tightly in her fists. Unexpectedly, pain exploded throughout the side of her head, filling her eyes with tears. Mommy had hit her.

"Go back to bed, you little shit," Tammy Bishop mumbled, rolling away from her. "Get out of here."

"But Mommy..."

The voices were frantic now, raising the level of terror coursing through Tory's small frame. Then she sensed him, the bad man, the one Mommy had said was her daddy. But she'd felt the evil rolling off him and knew Mommy had lied. Tory's daddy was a prince. Or an angel. Or maybe a princely angel. Just not the bad man.

She let the mist guide her into the hall closet and burrowed under a blanket that had been thrown carelessly on the floor. Surrounding her, the mist obscured the blanket and her presence beneath it only moments before the front door of their little apartment crashed open. She slapped a hand over her mouth to conceal a tiny cry, tears beginning to slowly leak down her cheeks. The voices murmured softly, trying to soothe her, but it wasn't until heavy footsteps went unheeded past her hiding spot that Tory's immediate panic receded. And then the screams began.

Clasping her hands tightly before her, Tory began to pray to the angels. She didn't want to die and even though Mommy sometimes called her a baby, she wasn't. Tory knew if the bad man found her, he would kill her. And so she prayed until Mommy grew silent and the laughter began. The sound, one Tory knew she would never forget, chilled her to the bone. Her prayers were forgotten as pure terror filled her soul, squashing all that was good, all the hope and love within her, leaving her dejected and heartsick.

It called to her, trying to draw her into its evil web, and the only thing holding her back from answering was the mist. They saved her that night, the spirits drawn to her light, not releasing her from their otherworldly grip until all was silent and the veil of evil had lifted. Only then was Tory able to crawl out of the closet.

"Mommy?" she called as she slowly trudged down the hallway.

Coming to a stop outside Mommy's bedroom, the hands

tried to hold her back, but she slipped right through their grasp. Their protection had weakened them and she had to see...had to know.

What filled her vision stunned her for one split second before high-pitched screams of horror were ripped from her throat. And while she shrieked, tears streaming down her cheeks, trails of her mother's blood slowly trickled down the walls.

Task completed, Asmodeus was enraged to find himself forced back within the human's circle. He should be free. He'd lived up to his end of the bargain. Now he should be able to collect the man's soul and be on his way, but he'd obviously been betrayed. He was going to enjoy killing the little pissant.

Centering his focus on the circle of protection, Asmodeus concentrated all his energy on the weakened spot until the spell fractured, leaving him free to cross the black line. The shocked look on the human's face filled him with eager anticipation. He could only hope the man ran. Nothing was as satisfying as hunting a target down.

"You can't do that! You have reneged on our deal. You promised me the bitch would die!"

To his great annoyance, the human did not flee. No, the sniveling little bastard held his ground, bitching and whining in the short span of time it took Asmodeus to reach him. He wrapped a fist around the man's neck and then lifted the sputtering weakling from the floor, leaving him dangling in the air, clutching at Asmodeus's wrist.

"How dare you question my vow? Your drugs made it too easy. The woman was hardly any challenge at all. There was little left for your authorities to identify."

"She is not dead," the human croaked out. "The child still lives."

The warlock's words stopped Asmodeus cold and he dropped the human like a sack of potatoes. Child? There hadn't been a child. And when he'd given voice to these questions, the man rose to his knees, his hands cradling his throat.

"The vision has not changed. Obviously the girl still lives."

Asmodeus cocked his head, considering the human's words. This time he would learn all of it. There would be no more mistakes. He would be no human's puppet. "What vision?"

"If the brat is allowed to live she will be the death of me."

A grin spread across Asmodeus's face. The fool. "She already is. You just don't realize it," he purred as a black Khopesh sword materialized in his hand. Fear had barely registered on the human's face when, after a broad sweep of his arm, the man's head began rolling across the floor. Inhaling deeply, he sucked the escaping soul into him, to be forever more trapped in torment. Oh, life was good.

Stepping over the body at his feet, Asmodeus set out to complete his mission. He had a girl to kill. Then he would be free.

Chapter One

Looking at the items around her, Victoria Bloom knew something was missing. She had the pentagram outlined in chalk on the old attic floor. At each point rested a large white candle, all of which was surrounded by a circle of protection. Ginseng burned on the makeshift altar, the scent so overpowering it almost gagged her. The *Grimoire of Armadel* was opened to the correct page. Ari, one of her spirit guides, insisted she was ready, but still she hesitated. The one thing Tory considered to be essential for the ritual to work was the very thing she lacked. Belief.

Funny really, considering Tory was a medium, meaning she saw ghosts, and she was preparing to perform an ancient ritual, all on the advice of a woman who had been dead for almost four centuries. But she couldn't deny something had to be done. On her twenty-fifth birthday, her powers had begun to emerge, powers her guides would soon no longer be able to camouflage. Calling forth an angel, though, seemed a little extreme, even for her.

"Hurry up," Ari whispered in Tory's mind. *"You don't have all day."*

"Yes, the spell must be performed before the sun sets. You don't want to accidentally call forth a demon, do you?" Sam prodded and Tory sighed. Sometimes she wondered what it would be like to be the only voice in her head.

"Boring," Thomas added, his nasal tone a reprimand. *"Now get the sigil drawn so we can get this over with."*

Tory snorted but didn't bother arguing. It wouldn't do her any good anyway. One of the three guides always seemed to have the last word.

In the center of the pentagram, she carefully copied the sigil from the ancient grimoire. The three stooges, something she had affectionately termed her guides when she'd been a child and continued because it annoyed them so much, had debated for days, poring over the book before finally coming up with a name. Tory would have picked the most powerful warrior to aid her but the stooges had been adamantly against her choice. It seemed even though Michael's mission was to protect humans, he didn't like them very much.

Setting the book aside, Tory picked up the dagger. With the stooges egging her on, she sliced the blade across her palm and gasped. It stung like a bitch. Eyes watering, both from the incense and the cut, she pressed her palm in the center of the sigil, leaving behind a bloody print. Then she moved out of the protective circle and began to chant, calling forth the angel Zadkiel. The words flowed from her, unknown and mysterious, a testament to how much power now flowed through her, energy Tory feared would be her downfall.

A blinding light burst forth within the center of the pentagram, causing her to draw a hand up to shield her eyes as the words faltered on her lips. Time seemed suspended. The rays illuminated every corner of the attic and Tory held her breath, fearing for the first time more than just the evil hunting her. As her body was enveloped within the white beams, she waited for the burn.

Slowly, the light dimmed and she was stunned to find herself unscathed. But still Tory hid her eyes behind her hand. Who knew what the hell stood on the other side. And since her father was, if the bastard still lived, a demon-worshiping warlock, hell was entirely possible.

"You foolish human. I was in the midst of an important meeting. Send me back. Now."

Her hand fell from her face, her gaze latching onto the figure in the middle of the pentagram. *Holy shit.* It had worked. And he was huge. Close to seven feet tall with long black hair cascading around broad shoulders and rippling biceps. His arms were folded across his massive chest, fists clenched in obvious agitation, causing the veins to bulge prominently.

Tory lifted her eyes to his face and the stark beauty she found there left her dumbfounded. He had a strong face, high cheekbones and a pronounced jaw presently ticking in anger. Ice-blue eyes framed by thick black lashes and full lush lips frowned down at her.

"Well?" he asked, arching one raven-hued brow.

"Please, Zadkiel, I am in desperate need of your help."

"Lord, save me from idiots. I am not Zadkiel, you nitwit."

"Oh shit," Ari muttered.

"What do you mean, oh shit?" Tory demanded. "What have you three gotten me into now?"

"Michael," came the whispered reply, and Tory knew she was in some serious trouble.

"Just what I need. A feeble-minded human. Can this day get any worse?" the angel mumbled, jerking her attention back to him.

"I am not feeble-minded," she cried indignantly, fear quickly forgotten. "And it would serve you right if Fate bit you on the ass."

Michael snorted. "Those three bitches know better than to mess with me. Now I have more important things, woman, than to share insults with you."

Tory watched him curiously, wondering what he thought he was going to do. His eyes closed and he seemed to be concentrating really hard on something. Several moments later, his face scrunched up, his eyes opening to pierce hers with an enraged glare. He took two giant steps forward, stopping inches from the edge of the protective circle. Tory held her breath, suddenly afraid it would not hold him, leaving her with one very pissed off angel on her ass. But Michael didn't try to step over the invisible barrier.

"Release me."

"I do not intend to hold you indefinitely as my own personal avenging angel." Tory watched in fascination as her statement caused his brow to arch again. Damn, but he was hot. It was such a shame he was a jerk.

"Then what are your intentions, human?"

"I have a name. It is Victoria Bloom, Tory for short."

"Your names are meaningless," he replied with an indifferent shrug. "Nothing better than cattle."

"Why protect us if you disdain humans so much?"

"What you have become disgusts me. The corruption. The greed. But that has nothing to do with why I hunt the fallen. There is no atonement for those who raised a sword against the Father and it is my job to terminate them."

"The fallen? You mean demons?"

Michael shook his head. "There are others who track and kill what you know as demons, the abominations created by Lucifer and Lilith. The fallen were once angels who rebelled and have been cast into Hell."

"Tell him," Ari whispered in her ear.

"Yes, tell him," Sam repeated, an annoying echo in her head.

"Asmodeus," Thomas added insistently.

"Who is Asmodeus?" Tory demanded. It was the first time any of the stooges had mentioned a name in connection with the demon who hunted her and she was pissed they had been hiding something so important all this time.

"Asmodeus?" Michael growled. "What does the Lord of Wrath have to do with why I've been brought here?"

Tory ignored the big bad angel, instead focusing her attention on the three stooges. "Someone had better start explaining. And quickly." Her belligerent tone could not be helped. Discovering she had been kept in the dark when her very life hung in the balance didn't have Tory feeling particularly magnanimous.

Ari ignored her. The spirit's awareness was completely centered on Michael, and neither Sam nor Thomas made a sound. Those two were never quiet. Especially Thomas. The cranky old bird had an opinion on everything.

"Is it that bad?" she whispered, swallowing convulsively around the words and fighting the bleakness slithering up her spine.

"Just who the hell are you speaking to?"

Tory flinched at Michael's demand. "My guides. They say the demon hunts me."

"Exactly how is this my problem?"

Wrapping her arms around her torso, Tory tried to fight off the chill sweeping the room at Michael's icy tone. The tiny kernel of hope she'd been secretly protecting since she'd discovered the truth of her birth withered and died. She should be used to it, having learned long ago no one gave a damn about her. At least no one living. So why the hell did it hurt so badly?

"I will release you." The words were forced out around the sob fighting for freedom, but Tory managed to hold back the tears.

Michael opened his mouth to speak but it shut with a definitive snap when an inhuman screech rent the air. The mist lapping at Tory's calves split, a portion swirling violently toward

Michael until stopping inches from the magical barrier it too could not cross. Stretching and lengthening toward the ceiling, it began to slowly transform until in its place stood the iridescent figure of a young woman.

"You conceited bastard," Ari shrieked. "You owe me."

Startled by Ari's appearance—the spirits rarely, if ever, showed their human form to Tory much less anyone else—it took Tory a moment for her outburst to sink in. It certainly sounded as if Ari had some familiarity with the angel but that couldn't be. Ari would have told her before she'd ever attempted this fiasco. Wouldn't she?

"Ariadne," Michael said softly.

The way he breathed out her name and the sheer fact he looked like he'd been run over by a Mack truck confirmed Tory was not the only one eating a big helping of betrayal. Never in a million years would she have believed any of her guides, but especially Ari, would dupe her in such a way. And why? For what purpose? Since Michael had appeared, Tory had felt like she was driving down a one-way street in the wrong direction. The stooges had been the only beings on Earth Tory had felt she could trust. Until now.

"You owe me," Ari repeated, this time at a whisper and Michael sighed heavily, searching Tory out with his eyes. She felt those blue orbs sweep over her frame, slowly, like phantom fingers reaching out to draw her close. Then Michael nodded.

"If you return to where you belong, I will deal with Asmodeus."

Ari glanced over her shoulder at Tory. Her face was etched with sadness and seemed to beg for understanding, but Tory found herself a little short on that emotion. Maybe if she'd had some clue as to what was going on... Hell, who was she kidding? She would have still been pissed had she known all the spirit had apparently been hiding from her.

"Your vow, Michael, and I will go."

175

Michael only hesitated for a second before nodding in acquiescence.

"The words. I am not foolish enough to believe you without the words."

As the angel's eyes narrowed in a mixture of anger and indignation, Tory was glad the piercing gaze was not aimed at her. She would have wet her pants. But Ari just rested her hands on her hips and waited.

"I vow I will deal with Asmodeus."

"And you'll protect Victoria. You, Michael. Not one of your little followers."

His fists clenched, released, then tightened again as he glared down at the apparition, and Tory fell back several steps. Baiting a pissed-off angel seemed like a really bad thing to do, and since she was the only other being in the room still living, Tory figured she would be the one to pay if Michael decided to come after someone.

"You have my vow," he practically snarled, seemingly not the least bit happy about Ari's demands. Not that Tory could blame him. She wasn't particularly pleased herself. The last thing she wanted to do was spend any more time in the angel's presence than absolutely necessary.

"Release the spell, Tory."

Her head shot up in surprise and she found Ari had turned toward her and was watching her solemnly. "Just like that? Without a word of explanation? I don't think so."

A ghostly hand reached out to caress her cheek. "It's the way it must be, baby girl. I can no longer protect you. But Michael can. And he will. It's time."

Stupidly, Tory shook her head. Time for what? She couldn't even form the words to ask. Ari had been with her for as long as Tory could remember, long before the death of her mother. She couldn't imagine a tomorrow without the spirit in it, even if her faith in Ari had taken a hit.

"I would never allow you to come to harm," Ari said softly, her ghostly gaze filling with unshed tears. "Release him."

Tory hesitated a moment, her mind trying to remember all the reasons why this was such a bad idea, before sighing as she reluctantly knelt at the edge of the circle. Using the blade still covered with her blood, she cut a line in the chalk, effectively breaking the protection spell. A powerful blast of energy hit her square on the chest, knocking her on her butt as she unconsciously drew the power back inside her body.

Towering over her like an avenging warrior, Michael held within his tight grasp a mighty sword, the likes of which Tory had never seen. The leather-wrapped handle had little adornment, only a leaf print etched in the silver base. Nothing really to remark over. The blade though was another story and had her frozen in disbelief. If one could actually call it a blade. The damn thing was a good three feet of red and orange flame swaying menacingly.

She was so dead.

Tory squeezed her eyes shut, hands over her head, waiting for a blow that never came. Instead, she heard Michael stride past her. Peeking from beneath her fingers, she watched for one surreal moment as he swung the blade of flame directly into the apparition that was her best friend. Then, with a flash of light and a loud popping sound, Ari was gone and Michael was standing over her again.

"What have you done?" Tory whispered, past caring she might anger him. There wasn't a damn thing she could do if Michael decided to take her life. She figured at least with the angel it wouldn't be the painful experience the demon hunting her would make of it.

"Get your ass into that circle and bespell it. I will return shortly."

Her jaw dropped. That was all Michael had to say to her.

Madelyn Ford

"Now just one minute—" Her sputtering came to an abrupt halt when Tory found herself in Michael's arms. But only for a second. Instead of dealing with any arguments from her, he'd scooped her up then dumped her in the middle of the pentagram.

"Why me?" he mumbled. Then one minute Michael was there and the next he was gone.

Chapter Two

Striding through the maze of intricate passageways, Michael wrestled to get his temper under control. He was leader of the Powers, an elite group of warriors originally formed to police their own kind but whose sole purpose was now hunting down and terminating those who joined Lucifer's ranks. He should have been immune to the trappings of humans. Or so he would have liked to believe. It was a valuable lesson born home by a tiny blonde he could have crushed with his bare hands if he'd been inclined. But he hadn't and it just pissed him off.

Instead, the need to draw her into his arms had slammed him in the chest. For the briefest moment, he'd actually felt his soul reach for hers. Michael had stopped that shit almost immediately. He'd seen what mating with a human had done to Gabriel. The death of Ariadne Duchesne had damn near destroyed him. In the four hundred years since she'd been slain, he and Gabriel had spoken maybe a couple dozen words and those had all been laced with hostility. At least from Gabriel's end. He blamed Michael for her death. It was why Michael had agreed to help the human. He wanted to make amends. Not because she made his dick harder than a spike and his soul cry with need.

"Big of you to grace us with your presence."

Michael folded his arms across his chest and arched a brow at his second in command, hardly amused by Zadkiel's sardonic drawl. Never mind Zadkiel had been the one Tory had been trying to summon. Tory... Best to forget about her with all that luscious blonde hair smelling of lilacs.

Shit. If he got a hard-on Zadkiel would never let him live it down.

"Maybe if you'd had something of interest to impart, I'd have stuck around."

"How's this, lord asshole? A report has come in from Skath. A witch managed to scry upon one of Lucifer's high-ranking lieutenants."

"Who?" Michael demanded, letting the asshole comment slide because when Lucifer's name was uttered in his presence, the rage flooding his system usually prevented him from concentrating on anything else. The knife his *once* best friend had quite literally embedded in his back was not something Michael had ever thought he would forget. Until today. Today the all-encompassing fury was replaced with something feeling suspiciously like fear.

Zadkiel cocked his head to the side, studying Michael for a moment and holding his breath. Michael waited for the smart-ass comment that never came.

"Asmodeus. He's somewhere in the Houston area."

As the air rushed from his lungs, Michael nodded, glancing away. If Asmodeus was in Houston he was far from Boston and Tory. "Gather a team and keep me informed. I want to know every move he makes before the bastard makes it."

"Michael, what's going on?"

Michael had turned to leave, wanting to gather a few things from his room before he returned to Tory, but Zadkiel's quiet question stopped him in his tracks. He sighed. It wasn't like he was particularly surprised. He didn't usually get involved in the hunt unless it was for one of the top-ten ruling archdemons. He commanded and his lieutenants followed. It was how things had worked before Ariadne had pulled him into this mess.

Before Tory.

"I have the chance to fix things with Gabriel. It's a long shot, but a shot nonetheless, and one I can't pass up."

"What? How?"

Michael smiled at Zadkiel's surprised excitement. He'd have shared Zadkiel's joy if only he didn't fear there was much more at risk than Gabriel's friendship. Michael suspected his entire way of life was in peril, his very soul in jeopardy.

"I believe I know what Asmodeus is after, but I do not understand why. There is a human he hunts, one I have vowed to protect." At Zadkiel's cocked eyebrow, Michael sighed. "It is a long story, but Ariadne's spirit had latched onto the human and it was to her I have given my vow. I can only hope once Asmodeus has been destroyed and the human's safety is ensured, my debt to Gabriel will have been repaid."

"Just like that?" Zadkiel questioned, his tone laced with skepticism.

Glancing over his shoulder, Michael shrugged. Truly, he doubted it, but it was the first chance he'd ever gotten to repair the mess with Gabriel. He suspected the only way he'd ever receive Gabriel's forgiveness was by experiencing the soul-crushing death of a mate. His mate. And Michael swore there wasn't a chance in hell of that ever occurring. His job did not include a mate, no matter what Victoria Bloom made him feel.

"Let me deal with this human, Michael. If you vowed to protect her, wouldn't it make more sense for you to lead the hunt? There is no one more capable."

Michael turned back to Zadkiel. Here was his chance. Though he had given his vow to Ariadne, technically since she was not the one who had called him into the circle, he was not required to uphold his end and he could send Zadkiel in his place. And his lieutenant was correct. Relations with humans were not exactly his forte. Hell, he'd probably end up doing more harm than good. So why did the thought of Zadkiel

181

anywhere near Tory make him want to hit something?

The answer was something Michael would rather not consider, though he knew. Deep in his heart, he knew.

"While nothing would give me greater pleasure, the vow I gave was very explicit. I must ensure Tory's protection."

"Tory?" Zadkiel repeated quietly and hearing her name on his lieutenant's lips reinforced Michael's belief. He was screwed with a capital S. He tightened his fists to keep from popping his second in the mouth.

"Care to elaborate?" Zadkiel glanced down at Michael's clenched fingers.

"No." And with that snarled pronouncement, Michael stormed from the room, taking the flight of stairs two steps at a time. Stopping only when the door to his bedroom was closed tightly behind him, he was glad he had not run into anyone else. Of course, the look on his face probably would have dissuaded even the most persistent. Well, except for maybe Raphael. He enjoyed tweaking Michael's temper for his own sadistic amusement, but since Raphael had no cause to be here Michael felt relatively safe. But just in case, maybe he should see about keeping Raphael busy for a while. Which lead his thoughts back to Tory. He definitely didn't need Raphael showing up in the middle this assignment.

Damn it. He didn't need this mess right now.

But the one thing Michael knew was there was no avoiding it. Few angels suspected the truth about mating, and the small minority who had found theirs believed themselves to be the exception. It was a lie, of course. Across time, across space, across dimensions, there was a soul mate out there for each one of them. Angels had been created with the capacity for great love, and what grander love existed than the unselfish bonding of two individuals?

Stuffing articles of clothing into a duffel, Michael tried to ignore the dismay that always overcame him when he considered those early days, when Earth had been discovered and some angels had set off to occupy the planet. It was then the first changes had begun, when Lucifer had first met Lilith, when the first visions of hell had been conceived.

Sighing, Michael zipped the bag closed. He'd fought it, strived to keep Lucifer and Lilith apart, just as he'd attempted to dissuade Gabriel away from Ariadne. But neither had listened to his misgivings, and he'd been right. Both instances had turned out disastrously. Now it seemed it was his turn. Would history repeat itself once again? Or would the Fates look more kindly upon him?

Doubtful. Those bitches hated him.

Raphael had once suggested bribing the trio. With chocolate. Shaking his head, Michael's lips formed into a small smile. Raphael was always unintentionally pissing them off and getting his ass burned in the process. Michael, on the other hand, had never cared one way or the other. Guess it helped the Fates were terrified of him.

Throwing the duffel over his shoulder, Michael left his room, wondering if this was the last time he would be gracing these four walls. Or was he destined to return a haunted shell like Gabriel?

Maybe he should pay the Fates a visit, see if Tory had crossed their notice. But then he decided that would just be asking for trouble. No need drawing attention if there wasn't any.

Exiting the Hall of Powers, Michael surveyed the landscaping making up Heaven. It was one of many different dimensions. There were others, like Hell, Fairie, Merwood and Earth, where humans and those with human origins could travel between, but it was believed the only entrance into Heaven for those earthbound was through death. Michael was one of the few who knew differently. It was another lie, propagated to prevent the fallen from attempting to surge the

Pearly Gates. If they could only find them. Finding the entrance to Heaven, that was the trick.

Michael and the rest of the angels were not tied to the Earth like their human counterparts, but aside from that fact, they had far more in common with the species then most would be willing to admit. Hell, humans were the children of angels, after all.

Damn Kronos and Rhea for starting this mess. If they'd kept their hands off each other he wouldn't be in his current position.

Shaking his head, Michael concentrated on his intended target, visualizing Tory before teleporting back to her. A moment passed as he tried to get his bearings. The small enclosure was hot and filled with a fine mist that obscured his vision. It took Michael those few seconds to determine where he was, and when he finally did the duffel slid from his fingers. Tory was before him, naked as the day she'd been born, standing under the spray of water, a clear glass door the only thing separating them.

For one split second, Michael wondered how long it would take him to strip off his clothes and join her.

Blonde hair, darkened by the flow of water, cascaded down a slender back, the ends coming to rest an inch or two above a tight, heart-shaped ass. His body tightened, his dick lengthening and hardening against the zipper of his jeans. Then Tory turned and Michael almost swallowed his tongue.

Dipping her head under the shower head, she arched her back, thrusting small, perky breasts into the air. Involuntarily, his hands rose, reaching for those mounds and the cherry-tipped nipples proudly on display. Barely taller than a pixie, Tory was mostly long sleek legs, legs he wanted wrapped around him.

Groaning softly, Michael clenched his fists, forcing them back down to his sides. What he wouldn't give to drop to his knees, burying his face in the blonde curls shielding her sex; to free his dick and sink into bliss. Harder than steel and pulsing with need, his dick more than agreed. But his brain, the sliver not blood deprived, recognized something was wrong with the scene before him, and he desperately clung to that thought.

Then it hit him.

"Why the hell aren't you where I left you, safe within the circle of protection?" he bellowed, causing Tory to let loose a shriek, her hands jerking in a vain attempt to shield her nakedness from his view. But her image had been burned into his mind and Michael already recognized what a lost cause it was. He would have her, of which there was no doubt. The question was would he be able to keep her?

Eyes wide, Tory stared at him, and Michael wondered if maybe he had been right when he'd first believed her to be dim-witted. It would just be his luck. There was little he found more irritating than stupidity and incompetence. His time with her would be doomed before it ever even began.

"Get me a towel," she finally snapped, and when he didn't jump to do her bidding, Tory added, "Now."

For such a little thing, she sure had balls.

"Well, don't just stand there."

Michael barely suppressed the grin from breaking free. "Maybe if you asked nicely I would be more inclined to do your bidding. Otherwise, I can continue to enjoy the view."

Michael was pretty certain he could hear her teeth grinding from across the bathroom. "Please."

"Oh, you can do better than that," he purred in delight as her eyes narrowed. Apparently she was neither stupid nor timid, just in need of training, and Michael was more than up for the challenge.

"Please," Tory repeated, her softer, breathier tone going straight to his dick.

Michael reached for the towel resting on the edge of the sink before moving across the small space, stopping out of her reach, forcing Tory to leave the confines of the shower stall and come to him. Then, instead of handing it to her, Michael wrapped the towel around her shoulders. His fingers lingered over her satiny skin, sliding down her arms as his gaze held hers.

Desire leapt between them, her eyes darkening under his steady perusal. Michael couldn't resist bending his head, capturing her lips gently. A soft moan escaped her, parting her lips and allowing his tongue access to the wet cavern. With a slow sweep, Michael tasted Tory, a mixture of honey and vanilla, a taste he could easily become addicted to.

As the flame burned bright, licking across his skin in waves of intense heat, the kiss grew demanding, and Michael pulled Tory against him, her damp skin clinging to his T-shirt, her puckered nipples grazing his chest. It took every ounce of control Michael had not to bend his head and suck one of those little beads into his mouth.

Dragging his lips from hers, Michael moved to her ear, capturing the lobe between his teeth before whispering, "Why did you leave the protective circle, Tory?"

"Because it is daylight," came her fevered reply, and Michael couldn't fault her reasoning. Demons were unable to tolerate the sun. It burned them to ashes. But while he couldn't fault her reasoning, he didn't have to like it.

"If you and I are going to work, when I tell you to do something, you must obey, Tory. No arguments. You must do what you are told."

Tory jerked away from him and the loss of her in his arms hurt—far more than Michael would have ever expected. When he moved to draw her back, she skirted out of his reach.

Chapter Three

"You arrogant pig," Tory snarled, avoiding Michael's attempt to drag her back into his arms. What had she been thinking, rubbing against him like a cat in heat? He'd more than made his position blatantly clear. He was there for one reason and one reason only, because Ari had forced a pledge out of him. Had she no pride?

With her body screaming for Michael to finish what he had started, obviously not.

"Don't come near me," she scolded when Michael tried to follow her.

"Then cover yourself," he snapped.

Tory felt her face flushing with embarrassment. In her great haste to do as ordered, Tory almost lost the tentative hold she had on the towel. She finally managed to shift it from her shoulders, securing it tightly under her arms while glaring defiantly at him.

"I was in the shower. And you were not invited."

"You were not where I had left you." Bending, Michael retrieved a black duffel bag from the floor, and after one last sweeping glance over her, he turned toward the door. "Get dressed," he demanded over his shoulder. "Then we'll talk."

Tory made a face as the door slammed behind him. Arrogant prick. But she couldn't help noticing the bulge that had clearly been outlined in his dark jeans. It kind of surprised her. She hadn't expected angels to be susceptible to desire.

With the towel still clutched tightly between her breasts, she had no choice but to follow him from the bathroom. She hadn't brought any clothing into the bathroom when she'd decided to shower. She hadn't known she'd need to.

"Love, you are playing with fire. Quit tempting me and cover your delectable ass or you will find yourself flat on your back."

Tory knew her mouth was hanging open and she lashed out to cover her unease. "Tempt you? I'd sooner rut with a donkey."

She watched with a weird sense of fascination as Michael arched a mocking brow before slowly stalking her across the room. Tory hadn't even realized she'd been retreating with each step he took until her back hit the wall behind her. She was totally at his mercy now, trapped by his body. His chest pressed against hers, drawing a soft gasp from her lips.

"Would you care for me to disprove your statement? Because I would be more than happy to, love," he whispered, his lips inches from her own and there was something wholly dangerous about his tone. Excitement skittered across her skin.

"I didn't think angels were interested in sex," Tory breathlessly said, arching her neck to avoid contact with his lips, knowing if he kissed her again, she would beg to make his promise reality. And Tory didn't need any more complications. Her life was disastrous enough without falling in love with an angel. Deep down she sensed there would be ramifications for such an act. She was human after all, and Michael wasn't.

"We aren't. Not unless it's with our mate." Michael stiffened for a second, frowning down at her, and Tory got the distinct impression he hadn't meant to voice that out loud. He lowered his arms, moving back enough for her to gain release, but still she stared at him wide-eyed. Rubbing the back of his neck, he turned from her and moved toward the window. "Get dressed,

Victoria."

He sounded in pain and Tory took a step toward him before she even realized she had done so. She halted, sighing softly. A strong impulse tugged at her, the need to give Michael comfort, but she didn't understand it and suspected he wouldn't accept it. She needed him to kill a demon. She shouldn't expect anything else because she would only end up getting hurt.

After escaping into the closet, Tory quickly dressed, hardly giving any consideration to what clothing she slipped over her body. Her comfy jeans and an old BU sweatshirt. She recognized her need for the familiar as a form of protection. But against Michael or her own fanciful inclinations? A psychologist would have a field day with her issues.

Michael was exactly were she had left him when she exited the closet, staring intently out the bedroom window. She waited for him to say something, turn toward her, acknowledge her presence—anything, and when he didn't, she snapped.

"You wanted to talk, so talk."

Michael glanced over his shoulder, a slight smile on his lips. "Where are your spirits?"

Tory shrugged, surprised not only by his question but by the fact she hadn't heard a peep from either Sam or Thomas since her spell bringing Michael to her had gone haywire. "They're around here somewhere."

Michael nodded, glancing back out the window a moment before finally turning to face her. "And how long have you been able to see the dead?"

Tory lifted her shoulders again carelessly. "I hear them more than I actually see them. And they have been around for as long as I can remember. Since I was a child."

"Who was the witch, your mother or your father?"

His question raised memories Tory would just as soon forget. The truth of who and where she came from was something she had spent years wishing she could change. It was knowledge she still had not come to terms with, but unfortunately she knew she had to reveal because she suspected it had everything to do with why she was now being hunted.

"I don't remember much about my parents. They both died when I was five. My mother was a drunk but totally human. My father, or at least the man my mother had claimed was my father, was..." Her voice faltered, too embarrassed to ever give voice to the disgusting truth. Wrapping her arms around her torso, she sank onto the edge of the bed.

"Was what?" Michael asked quietly.

"Ari said he was a warlock," Tory confided and flinched, waiting for his reaction. She knew as an angel Michael couldn't help but be disgusted. Witches were white spell casters, men and women who devoted their lives to doing good. Warlocks were the complete opposite. Filled with greed, they aided demons in their evil work for profit and gain, intentionally giving up their souls in the process. They were everything angels despised.

"Was he under the command of Asmodeus?"

Surprised by the lack of revulsion in Michael's voice, Tory jerked her gaze up, shocked to find him kneeling at her feet. He lifted a hand, his fingers reaching out to gently stroke her jaw before cupping the back of her neck.

"I truly do not know. My father had little use for me or my mom, only coming around when he needed something, probably sex, I really do not remember. But even at four or five, I knew there was something wrong with him, so my guess would be yes, he was under Asmodeus's command. He felt evil."

"Can you still? Sense this evil in individuals, I mean?"

"And goodness," she said with a nod. "It has gotten stronger in the last couple of months. It was why Ari insisted I call forth an angel. She believed this extrasensory perception will soon be mutual, and that this demon will finally be able to find me."

Michael's facial features seemed to freeze in place and he snarled, "How long has he been hunting you?"

Tory, surprised by the rage dancing in his eyes and the flexing muscle in his jaw, shrugged. "I never knew until recently he even existed. The three stooges managed to hide all knowledge of him from me as effectively as they had hid me from him."

"What of spell casting? I can feel the power in you. Have you not thought to use a spell?"

Tory rolled her eyes. Did he think she was stupid? Then she recalled the times he had said as much. *Asshole.* "Yes, I've tried every spell I have been able to get my hands on. None of them have worked, but it's not exactly like I've had anyone to teach me this shit. There's only been Ari, Sam and Thomas."

"Yes. A hunter, a theologian and a banker. I'm sure they were a hell of a lot of help," Michael drawled, his voice dripping with sarcasm.

"Well, it's not like anyone else was going to step up to the plate," she stated, annoyed by his arrogance. It was her family Michael was talking about. An odd family, she would give him that, but the only one she'd ever known. "I didn't have a flock of angels at my disposal."

Michael dragged her closer as he leaned in. "You should have. If I'd known..." Shaking his head, he let his hand fall away before rising to his feet and striding to the other side of the room.

Tory needed to change the subject. Feeling as if they were standing on the edge of a steep cliff with a painful fall imminent, she picked something she thought would be safe...at least safer than where they had been heading. While she didn't know exactly where that might be, she feared it enough to want to avoid it. "Where is Ari? What did you do to her?"

Michael was silent a moment, disappointment etched across his face. With a sigh, he followed the direction she'd gently nudged the conversation. "I returned her to the Hall of Souls where she belongs."

Biting her lip, Tory wondered if she would have the nerve to ask what she was really dying to know—how Ari was connected to Michael. It wasn't really any of her business, and maybe if she kept telling herself that it would eventually sink in.

Or not.

"Whatever it is, ask it of me."

Michael sounded eager, too eager for the jealous rampage she wanted to embark upon. Who'd have thought she'd be envious of a dead woman, but apparently she was. And feeling very territorial over an angel she had absolutely no business even considering.

"How did you become acquainted with Ari?" *Okay, so I'm a fool,* Tory freely admitted to herself.

Michael's eyes grew vacant, as if he were immersed in a past memory. It took everything in her not to jump up and stomp from the room in an ill-tempered fit. Lord, she could just imagine his shock at that.

Appearing to be waking from a stupor, Michael blinked, his vision clearing. "She had been no more than a child, only nineteen when Gabriel introduced us," he said with a tinge of sadness.

Nausea settled in the pit of her stomach, but instead of demanding what the hell Ari had meant to him, she asked, "Who is Gabriel?" Because truthfully she was too big a wimp to find out.

Michael's eyes narrowed. "You know who he his, but are you sure you really want to discuss this? You might not like where it leads."

Tory didn't reply right away. Instead she recognized the

challenge in his eyes and his words and tried to determine the meaning behind them. Did Michael already know the feelings he seemed to raise in her? Was he warning her from the truth, knowing how badly it would hurt her? Or was it something else entirely?

She was about to demand an answer from him but Michael beat her to the punch.

"*The* Archangel Gabriel. Ariadne was his mate."

Mate? Michael had mentioned it before but what did he mean?

Tory would have verbalized the thought if not for Michael's sudden movement. He grabbed her arm, yanking her from the bed and shoving her behind him as a bright flash of light engulfed the room. Glad for his back shielding her, she buried her face in his shirt, hiding from what that light might entail. She wasn't worried it might be a demonic presence. It was still daylight out, and for some reason she figured demons would not cast such a pure white glow when they entered a room.

"What the hell are you doing here, Zadkiel?" Michael demanded, causing her curiosity to get the better of her. Tory peeked over his shoulder and shuddered.

Michael had brandished that beast of a sword again, but it wasn't the weird blade of flame that had caught her attention. It was Zadkiel. Tall, though not as tall as Michael, he stood before them, light brown hair brushing against broad shoulders and framing a face most women would have swooned over. But not Tory. Maybe if she hadn't seen Michael first... No, this angel didn't have her heart hammering and her mouth watering.

Her obvious preference for Michael couldn't be good.

A few mumbled words from Michael in what Tory thought might have been Latin and the sword disappeared, but he didn't relax his stance. It didn't take a genius to figure out he was not happy about the other angel's presence. Was it because of her? Or for some other reason?

"You wanted to be kept aware of Asmodeus's movements. I'm here to comply."

Chapter Four

Michael rolled his eyes. Sure he was. Zadkiel could have found another way to deliver a message of this importance, but it was Michael's own fault for mentioning Tory. He should have known Zadkiel would never be able to overcome his curiosity, and the way she clung to him would only further fuel Zadkiel's interest. Completely aware of every inch of Tory plastered against his back, Michael knew the wise thing would have been to push her away, but he couldn't do it. The way Zadkiel was eyeing her inflamed the need to draw her even closer, directly into the protection of his arms. Wouldn't that intrigue his second-in-command beyond imagination?

"So make me aware," Michael snapped, watching Zadkiel flicker a glance over his right shoulder, landing without a doubt on Tory. He could almost see the wheels turning behind his second's brown orbs. Zadkiel wanted to ask about Tory but thought better of it.

Michael hadn't made Zadkiel his second because he was stupid.

Zadkiel cleared his throat. "Asmodeus is on the move, leaving a trail of dead bodies in his wake. Powerful witches, every single one of them, and interestingly enough, all bear a striking resemblance to your...companion."

Tory's quiet gasp filled Michael's ears though it was the gentle trembling running along his spine that fully caught his attention. He hadn't wanted Zadkiel's notice directed at Tory any more than necessary, but the shudders racking her slight frame drew him and Michael turned, gathering her into his arms, completely aware of Zadkiel's probing gaze.

"It's my fault," she whispered, burying her face in his chest.

"Nonsense. You do not control Asmodeus's actions anymore than I." Michael cupped the back of her head to hold her close, his fingers sinking into wet hair. Lifting her face, he rested his forehead against hers. "Go dry you hair, love, before you get sick."

Tory hesitated only a moment before whispering, "Okay."

Michael knew her acquiescence was due to the fact she was upset. By the time she finished doing as he'd commanded she'd have her emotions under control and would no doubt come out claws drawn.

Watching her disappear into the bathroom—hell, he couldn't tear his eyes from Tory's retreating figure. It was only Michael's iron-willed control preventing him from dragging her back into his arms. It amazed him how quickly she'd become embedded in the very fiber of his being.

"Love?" Zadkiel questioned, forcing Michael's attention back to his second and the smirk plastered across his face. Frowning, Michael took a threatening step toward him, but Zadkiel only added, "Not quite the big scary archangel now that I've really seen how you treat humans."

"You will show some respect to my mate," Michael snarled before his brain caught up with the anger consuming him. Zadkiel's eyes widened and Michael cursed. That was the last thing he'd wanted to admit to anyone.

"Shit. You're sure?" At Michael's arched brow, Zadkiel nodded. "Of course you are. Now I understand why this has become such a priority. Any idea why Asmodeus is after her?"

"No, all I have is conjecture. Tory believes her father was a warlock, which explains the power she is coming into. And as

I'm sure you have noticed, what she has, she has in abundance. So I have two theories. Either her father made a blood pact with Asmodeus, and the bastard believes Tory, as his only descendant, is responsible for fulfilling it. Or he knows she is coming into her power and thinks to take it for his own. But I will not allow him to succeed."

"Well, of course not. And it won't hurt giving her a little Ambrosia."

Michael snorted, turning his back on Zadkiel. Ambrosia, nectar of the gods. Little could Homer have known how literal such a statement was when he'd coined the phrase all those centuries ago. And completely against the laws of Heaven.

"I will hardly be able to enforce a law I have myself broken."

"Neither can we afford for you to end up like Gabriel," Zadkiel said quietly. "I do not see how you have any choice."

Yes, he could justify the action that way, but it still would not make it any less wrong. Ambrosia was nothing but a pretty word for angel blood. Quite by chance, many millenniums ago, it had been discovered a few drops could make a human immortal. But too much had devastating effects, turning the human into an abomination. A vampire. Even Gabriel had feared the consequences, never taking such drastic steps to prolong Ariadne's life.

Though maybe he should have because the thought of losing Tory the way Gabriel had Ariadne twisted deep in Michael's gut. He wasn't sure he could be so noble.

A wave of gut-wrenching remorse swept over him and Michael instantly recognized from where it had come. Tory. She needed him.

"We both have our own responsibilities. Yours is tracking Asmodeus. Mine is taking care of the woman in there," Michael said, waving a hand toward the bathroom door. "Let me know if you discover anything new, but right now I need to concentrate on Tory."

He didn't bother to wait for a reply. In his desperate need to reach her, he just left Zadkiel standing there. It was vexing really. Had it been any one of his warriors, Michael would not have hesitated reprimanding for such an action. But the shoe was on the other foot now, and Michael could not deny he was operating in ways completely out of character for him.

Michael found Tory sitting on the toilet seat, arms wrapped tightly around her waist, and though she didn't make a sound, tears streamed slowly down her cheeks. His heart lurching, he hesitated only a moment, uncertain how he should proceed as he watched her rocking slowly back and forth. What did he know of easing a human's pain? Hell, what did he know of offering comfort to anyone?

But she was his mate.

Kneeling before her, Michael did not even think she realized her actions when she leaned into him. It was the most natural thing in the world to gather her into his arms. The one thing he'd feared had become the most treasured.

He'd be breaking one of his people's oldest covenants by feeding her Ambrosia. In that, Michael knew he had no choice. He only prayed his motives would be deemed pure enough to be forgiven.

Settling on the floor, he shifted Tory onto his lap, cradling her against his chest, surrounding her with his warmth. She sank into him, giving her weight up into his protection and that measure of trust twisted something inside Michael, invoking a feeling he'd never encountered. *Could this be love?*

He closed his eyes, relishing the feel of Tory in his arms. He still wanted her. His dick had grown hard the minute he'd stepped into the bathroom, but this was different. The harsh bite of arousal was gone. It was more subtle and not wholly unpleasant. Murmuring into her hair, he rocked her gently until her trembling began to subside and she finally grew still.

"We will find him," Michael said quietly.

At first a sniffle was the only reply. Then in a whisper, Tory asked, "But how many more will die because of me?"

"My love, you have no more control over life and death than do I. Who's to say it wasn't their time? And they are in a better place."

"Are they? Really?"

"I would like to think so. They are at peace. No more suffering, no more pain."

Tory snorted. His kitten was getting back her claws.

"But no life. You're just dead?"

"It is a different reality, love, but still an existence."

"Will you tell me about it?" she asked, her tone filled with a longing that tugged at Michael's heart strings. If he got his way, death would be something she'd never experience. Not first hand, at least.

"Later. But for now I want you to rest. We will need to be prepared once darkness falls. We might not know Asmodeus has found you until he is upon us, and I do not want you encumbered by fatigue."

Tory did not argue, which Michael saw as verification of her exhaustion. Nor did she utter a protest when he rose with her held tightly against his chest and left the bathroom. Ever so gently, he laid her on the bed then followed her down, unwilling to relinquish the feel of her body next to his. And it would make what he planned that much easier.

Grimacing against the pain, Michael bit down on the top of his tongue hard enough to draw blood. As the honeyed taste filled his mouth, he lowered his head, his lips covering Tory's. Then, running his tongue along the seam of her lips, he tried to coax a response, to no avail.

Framing her face with his hands, he whispered, "Open for me, love." Gently applying pressure on her chin with his thumbs, he was filled with jubilant triumph when she complied.

Michael groaned as her tongue tangled with his before sweeping inside her mouth, making certain his essence mingled with her saliva.

What he would have given to get lost in Tory's arms, but he couldn't risk her consuming too much of his blood. Michael pulled back, his breath see-sawing from his lungs, his dick throbbing with unfulfilled desire. Glancing down, his eyes met green ones brimming with tears and it was like a punch in the gut.

"Tory?"

"I know I'm nothing more than an imposition, a vow forced upon you by Ari, but please don't leave me," she whispered, tripping over the words as one tear slid slowly down her cheek.

Brushing away the offending wetness with his thumb, Michael stared dumbstruck, only realizing he'd taken too long to respond when, with what sounded like a soft sob, Tory attempted to push him away. But refusing to budge, he pinned her squirming body to the mattress with his hips nestled between her thighs and her breasts pressed firmly against his chest. Her lush heat burned him through his jeans, cradling his dick with the promise of paradise. The vow to Ari was one Michael could definitely get behind.

"Ari does not belong here in our bed, Victoria. Now or ever."

Michael didn't know what reaction he had expected from his mate, but her hand connecting with his cheek was not one of them. It completely blindsided him, allowing Tory to push him off her and gain her freedom.

"Then where does she belong, Michael? Because I got the feeling you two were awfully close."

For one stunned moment, Michael tried to come to terms with the words Tory had snarled at him. Standing beside the bed, fists clenched in jealous anger, she was a sight to behold, revving up his desire a notch or two to where the only thing that mattered was getting her back under him. Then the implication of her insidious taunt sunk in. He must have misunderstood her meaning.

"Exactly what are you accusing me of, Tory?" he demanded quietly.

Chapter Five

Tory swallowed heavily. The pain lining Michael's face hit her full force in the chest, frightening her with the urgent desire to return to his arms, to ease the hurt she'd caused. Stumbling back a step, she refused to give in to the need. He could easily be playing her. For all she knew, Michael could be a real Casanova, his one and only desire to get into the pants of every woman he encountered. Though her body was screaming he was different, that what was between them was special, Tory was short on trust, and at present her faith in her own intuition was in short supply.

"Did you betray Gabriel? Is that why you feel such guilt over Ari's death?"

"Guilt? You think I what, fucked Gabriel's mate and once he discovered the truth he killed her?"

Blue eyes filled with rage centered on her, making Tory want to slink off into a corner and hide. It took every ounce of fortitude to hold her ground, to shrug her shoulders nonchalantly like the prospect of Michael's affirmation wouldn't destroy her.

Michael took a deep shuddering breath, rolling from his lounging position on the bed to sit on the edge of the mattress. Elbows centered on his thighs, his hands ripped through his hair before coming to rest on the back of his neck, his gaze locked firmly on the floor. "You know nothing of mates," he stated quietly. "But soon that will all change."

Michael's head lifted and Tory read the promise in his eyes. She turned to flee, only to be caught in the steely grip of his arms wrapping around her, her back braced against his chest. Squirming in an attempt to gain her freedom only seemed to make him more determined to keep her prisoner. His hold tightened as a set of teeth sunk into the tendons where her neck met her shoulder. The bite wasn't hard enough to draw blood but it drew a primitive instinct in her and Tory relaxed against him with a shudder.

"I do feel responsible for Ariadne's death," Michael whispered, his lips gently kissing away the sting of his bite. "But not in the way you think, love."

Michael's arms slid away from her. He stepped back and, with some reluctance, Tory allowed him to turn her. She wasn't entirely certain she wanted to face him, afraid of what she would read there. It would take an idiot not to have noticed the guilt smoldering in his blue orbs every time Ari's name was mentioned.

His hand caressed her cheek, leaving a trail of goosebumps as his fingers slid slowly down her neck and arm, stopping only when he reached her hand. Entwining their fingers, he led Tory to the bed, giving her arm a quick tug, sending her tumbling to the mattress next to him. With his body turned toward her, Michael drew her palm to his lips, placing a kiss in the center before pinning her hand over his heart.

"Many factors led up to Ariadne's death, so I will only give you the basics. But none of it had to do with betraying Gabriel. When Gabriel asked that I allow her to be trained as one of my hunters, I agreed for purely selfish reasons. The lifespan of a human hunter is not long and in the woman's death, I saw Gabriel's freedom." Michael gave a harsh bark of laughter. "How naïve I was thinking Gabriel would continue on as if she had never existed."

The look of anguish on Michael's face shattered the place deep inside her where fear and distrust had long resided. She cupped his cheek with her free hand, exalting in the way he leaned into her touch as if she had the power to heal him. It would only be fitting since he'd managed to free her from the baggage she'd been carrying since childhood.

"Hunting demons is a dangerous business. You can hardly be blamed for Ari's death."

"It is not her death putting a wedge between Gabriel and me. It's what I said later, the callous words I spoke for which he has never forgiven me. And I cannot blame him."

"What did you say?" Tory probed gently, but Michael only shook his head.

"I do not want you to hate me too," he whispered.

"That will never happen," she stated, her voice filled with absolute conviction. She didn't think there was anything he could say to change how she felt about him. Not that she wanted to examine too closely what her feelings were. Tory wasn't ready to admit them even to herself.

Unable or unwilling to meet her gaze, Michael stared down at their joined hands and Tory thought he wasn't going to respond. Then he spoke, so softly Tory had to strain to make out the words.

"I told him he was better off without the human to distract him. There were plenty of females with which he could scratch an itch. He didn't need Ariadne."

"Ouch," Tory murmured, wondering how Gabriel had taken such a pronouncement. Probably not very favorably.

"How the hell was I to know?" Michael cried. With a growl, he attempted to pull away from her, to put some distance between them, but Tory feared if she released the tight grip on his hand she would lose whatever was growing between them.

"How were you to know what?" Tory demanded.

"How the hell was I to know my mate would complete me in ways I'd never even suspected I needed?"

With those harshly snarled words, Michael crushed Tory to him, his lips demanding entrance, which she immediately gave. His tongue swept into her mouth, drawing a moan from her throat. Clothing was tossed aside with little finesse, the urgency having taken hold of Michael, leaving Tory feeling a little lost as he pushed her flat on the mattress, rising over her.

He brushed her hair from her face as his gaze swept over her slowly. "Christ, you're beautiful. My mate. My love."

Her breathing hitched, his words filling her with wonder. But Tory had little time to contemplate as Michael once again lowered his head, his lips devouring her own. His cock was there nestled between her thighs, and she waited impatiently for him to thrust into her body. Instead, he dragged his lips from hers, sliding down her body to surround a nipple in the moist heat of his mouth.

A cry slipped free as she arched her back, silently demanding more. She wanted harder, faster, anything to quench the flames licking at her insides. To her great dismay, Michael released the tight bud, chuckling softly. Her fingers embedded in his hair, trying to tug him back, only to have a sob forced from her throat when he moved to her other breast, his lips surrounding the nipple, his tongue lashing at the tip.

Not abandoning her other breast completely, his fingers tugged at the wet nipple, pulling and pinching until Tory thought she would lose her mind. Or orgasm just from his lips and fingers at her breasts. She arched her hips, searching for some form of relief, only to cry out at the feel of his hand sliding between her thighs. Fingers swept through the blonde curls and wet folds shielding her sex, moving to circle the opening of her vagina with the lightest of touches before sinking his fingers slowly inside.

"Damn, you're so wet," Michael murmured, his warm breath tickling her breast. "And tight. I won't last five seconds inside you, love."

Tory might have demanded he get to it before she died of unfulfilled lust but at that moment his thumb brushed her clit and she lost the ability to breathe much less think rationally. One finger then two drove through unused tissues, scissoring inside her pussy, stretching her. Understanding the semantics of sex, she still was not prepared for the unbelievable pleasure coursing through her veins. Her hips lifted and a sob tore from her throat as she met his swallow thrusts, wanting—no, needing deeper penetration. It was there just out of reach, and she wanted her damn orgasm.

One last lick to her tortured nipple and Michael was sliding down her torso. Tory tried to stop him but he slipped from her grasp. His lips lingered here or there, sucking lightly on her skin before continuing his journey. His broad shoulders forced her thighs farther apart, and to her horror he stopped, his face inches from her pussy. Reflexively, she attempted to close her legs, embarrassment flooding her as he seemed to be studying her sex.

Broad hands held her open, his thumbs spreading the folds so he could get a more intimate view. Tory would have surely protested his perverse interest if his tongue hadn't swept over her pussy, lingering on her clit and ripping a cry from her lips. Shit, she'd never expected such pleasure... Then his lips sucked her clit into his mouth and Tory detonated into a million little pieces.

She was still jerking and twitching from the most amazing climax when Michael rose over her, his erection poised at her entrance. His hands framed her face, his eyes capturing hers and he whispered, "Mine. My mate. Do you understand, love?"

And though Tory had no idea what the hell he was going on about, she nodded.

With a look of supreme satisfaction, he slowly began to work his cock inside her, his muscles tense under her fingertips, and Tory knew he was holding back for her. When he came to the membrane shielding her womb, the proof of her virginity, his eyes held a mixture of surprise and extreme arrogance.

He pulled her closer, his lips hovering over hers. "Hold on to me tightly, love. It will be over in a minute." Then he thrust forward, his lips capturing her soft cry. But it wasn't pain bringing tears to her eyes, it was the sense of fullness, of not knowing where she ended and Michael began, of being one.

"I'm sorry," he whispered, brushing away the tears from her face.

"Damn you," she whimpered. "You made me fall in love with you."

A brilliant smile encompassed Michael's face. "It's only fair since you made me love you first."

With a sniffle, a grin broke through her tears. "You better or I'll never forgive you."

"No fear there, love. Forever."

Then his hips retreated and thrust forward. Tory's eyes closed at the extreme rapture filling her. Wrapping her legs around his waist, she tried to hold onto the tidal wave swirling around her, but each plunge of his hips speared his cock deeper, harder, drawing her further into its murky grip, only to come crashing over her, sucking the breath from her lungs.

Michael's fingers dug into her flesh, angling her hips to penetrate impossibly deeper until with a harsh growl, he stilled, his cock head nudging the entrance of her womb. He tensed, soaking her hidden depths with blasts of semen and triggering another stellar orgasm from which she was sure she'd never recover.

Tory was still shaking from the intensity of their joining when Michael collapsed on top of her, burying his face in her neck. Clinging to him as if she feared he would disappear—and maybe a small part of her did—she recognized somehow the sex with Michael had been different. Sure, she'd been a virgin, but she read and watched movies. At the moment of climax it had felt like her soul had escaped the bounds of her flesh and had connected with Michael's. Even now, it was as if she could still feel him. She was pretty certain *that* was not normal.

Having every intention of demanding an explanation or two, Tory decided to wait until after she'd finished basking in her afterglow. In Michael's arms, she felt treasured, safe. And warm, he was like a giant furnace. Yes, she would want answers. Later.

Chapter Six

Leaning up on his elbow, Michael was amazed to find watching Tory sleep filled him with contentment. Slowly, he traced a finger over the swell of her hip, fascinated at the feel of her skin. It was like silk. And when he had been encased tightly within her body, it was like basking in the white light of Heaven.

Who would have thought he'd become ensnared in a human's web? Now he had to figure out a way to keep her.

Clenching his hands at the disturbing thought, he recognized he would need to devise a plan of action. There was no way in hell he was going to share Gabriel's fate, and even more importantly, neither would Tory share Ariadne's. He'd fight all the forces of Heaven and Hell to prevent it from happening.

Michael sighed. Soon the sun would be setting and darkness would fall. He should get her up but he hated to disturb the peace. After making love Tory had quickly succumbed to sleep, saving him from having to answer the questions he'd glimpsed lurking in her eyes. How was he to tell her she would need to leave everything she'd ever known to be with him? Because he couldn't let her go.

"What time is it?" Tory asked, pulling him from his musings.

His fingers curled around her hip, pulling her body flush

with his. "Just a little after six," he murmured against her lips before brushing them with his own. Her soft little moan had his dick hardening and if he hadn't had a demon to worry about, Michael would have given his mate a proper hello.

Instead, Michael forced himself to roll away from her. When it came to Tory, he was quickly realizing he had little to no control and the last thing he wanted was Asmodeus to come calling while he had his dick sunk deep within her pussy. Talk about getting caught with your pants down. It forced a smirk to settle on his face as he reached for his jeans and then slipped them over his legs and hips.

His name, gently whispered from Tory's lips, drew his attention back to his mate. "What is it, love?"

She was biting her bottom lip, her gaze apprehensive, and Michael knew whatever was on her mind would likely make him uncomfortable.

"We need to talk," she said quietly, and he knew he'd been right.

"We will, Tory. But first we need to dress. It is almost dark and Asmodeus could strike at any moment. We need to be prepared."

She studied him a moment and Michael wasn't certain Tory would concede to his demands. It wasn't like he had any compunction in forcing her to do his bidding. Hell, he'd throw her naked ass in the circle of protection she'd drawn if he thought for a second she'd stay there. If he only knew where the damn portal was, he'd take her to Heaven and never have to worry about the bastard harming her again.

Jerking a T-shirt over his head, Michael realized at first light he'd have to start a hunt of his own. He had to find the entrance to Heaven.

He pivoted then came to a swift stop when he realized Tory was right there anxiously watching him. She was already wearing the same jeans and sweatshirt he had stripped from her body not eight hours ago, and Michael longed to feel her naked skin plastered against his once again. Instead, he kissed her furrowed brow before stepping back lest he give into the temptation.

"All right, love. Let's talk, but not in here. Somewhere without a bed."

Glancing back at the object in question, he watched a little smile wash away the doubt on Tory's face. If it hadn't been like looking into a rainbow, Michael might have chastised her for her lack of faith. Instead he followed Tory from the bedroom, traveling down a narrow hallway to a steep staircase. At the bottom, in a small living room, he remained standing while Tory took a seat on the floral couch beneath the windowpane looking out onto the front yard. He watched her tug her bottom lip between her teeth, a habit he'd already come to associate with his mate's feelings of anxiety.

Her silence concerned him. Not wanting to take the chance she might try to flee, Michael took three cautionary steps closer until his shins rested against an old coffee table sitting in the middle of the room. There he stood, striving to wait for her to speak—she'd been the one who wanted to talk after all—but her hesitation quickly frayed Michael's nerves. "Tory?" he finally questioned, unable to remain silent any longer.

For a moment, he really thought she was going to completely ignore him. She refused to raise her head, her eyes fixed on her shoes, and Michael sighed. He was about to join her on the sofa when she spoke.

"Did you mean it?" she asked in a breathless rush.

Struggling to understand her question, he finally had to shake his head in confusion. "Mean what, love?"

Again Tory hesitated, and Michael's patience had come to an end. Sitting beside her, he lifted her head, forcing her eyes to meet his. Her bottom lip was once again captured between her teeth and, brushing a thumb over it, he encouraged her to set it free before she did any damage.

"Victoria, I cannot assuage your fears if I do not understand what they are."

"You said you loved me," came her quiet response, and he arched a black brow in confusion.

"And I do."

"But we only just met."

So that was what had his mate in a tailspin. Funny, he'd considered many things to explain her unease, but never her doubting his feelings. "If I recall, you were the first to declare such sentiment." Tory tried to glance away but Michael refused to release his hold, moving to frame her face with his palms. "I told you, Tory, you are my mate. I know for a human it can take longer, but for an angel it is instinctual. Our soul recognizes its other half almost immediately."

"But what if you are wrong?" she whispered and he sighed.

"Does it feel like I am?"

The denial, when it came, was not damn near quick enough for him. Michael couldn't believe they were having this conversation. He'd sensed her soul reach for his when they'd made love and he'd also felt his respond.

"Damn it, I'm not wrong," he answered, harsher than he'd intended. Tory tried to jerk away from him and he wrapped her in his arms in a silent apology, gentling his tone as he asked, "Didn't you feel it, love, our souls merging at climax, becoming one?"

"I thought..." Tory fell silent, hiding her face in his chest.

Michael's lips brushed the top of her head before rubbing his cheek against the silky strands of her hair. "You thought what?"

"I thought it was different but I wasn't certain."

He smiled into her blonde tresses, his arms reflexively tightening around her small frame. Tory had been a virgin so her confusion shouldn't have come as a surprise, but it had been centuries since Michael had even considered sex much less indulged in carnal relations. And still, he'd never lain with a human, only other angels. He couldn't honestly say he'd been expecting the bliss he'd found in Tory's arms.

Suddenly, he felt her stiffening against him. "Tory?"

"Michael, you have feared Gabriel's fate all this time and yet have found yourself in the same position. I am not immortal."

The little hitch in her voice should have had him rolling in guilt, only Michael found satisfaction in his ability to deny her statement. But how to tell Tory she would never die naturally? He had enacted a fundamental change in her very DNA without bothering to consult her.

Well, shit. "About that—"

Any other time, an interruption would have put Michael on edge, but this time he gladly welcomed the mist beginning to swirl around their feet and the nasally male voice whispering, "Damn. He's still here."

"Would you prefer he get a quick shag and run? Not with our girl."

"You do have a point, Samuel. However, I wouldn't have thought one of his kind would sink so low as to fornicate period."

"Must be the whole soul-mate thing. Never seen two souls merge like that before. Damn near blinded me."

Michael rolled his eyes. While he had been a bit busy at the time, he was still pretty sure he would have realized if either of the spirits had been in the room when he and Tory had been making love.

His mate, on the other hand, obviously believed the two— what had she called them—stooges. "You watched?" she squealed, lurching from his arms and jumping to her feet, confronting the two male spirits floating inches off the floor.

Michael sighed. While he was thankful for the distraction, the last thing he wanted was Tory upset by their presence.

"Well, of course we didn't watch," Sam reply indignantly. "Well...maybe some of it."

"Why you no good..." Tory snapped, taking a threatening step toward the spirits.

Wrapping his arm around her waist, Michael halted her progress, not at all certain exactly what she thought she was going to do. They were dead after all and impervious to most forms of torture. Except...

Michael's grip around Tory tightened, securing her to his side. With a few softly spoken words, his mighty sword appeared in his right hand. Pointing the fiery tip at the two ghosts, he watched in amusement as the mist danced about in a blatant attempt to avoid getting sucked into the flame.

"If neither of you would care to share Ariadne's fate, I suggest you stop annoying my mate."

Sam humphed loudly. "We were trying to help you out. Won't make that mistake again."

Michael grunted and the mist evaporated as if it had never been. Helping him, his ass. Those two were going to be trouble. He could feel it clear to the bone.

"Helping you? What was Sam talking about?"

Great. Trouble with a capital T.

"How the hell should I know, Tory? I do not think either of them is very stable. They should go to the light."

The last, which was spoken loudly just in case the two were still lingering about, caused a giggle to bubble from his mate's luscious lips, and Michael couldn't stop himself from sampling another taste.

"Well, shit. There is really something wrong with this sight. I think my retinas are fried," Zadkiel's amused drawl intruded.

Michael sighed as Tory jumped away from him. Turning to Zadkiel, he reminded himself taking off his second-in-command's head really wouldn't appease his annoyance. It would only reattach itself. And while it would hurt like a bitch, it would be far too temporary. No, instead he would give the other male courier duty. Let him spend a century ferrying messages from the lesser factions, like the Fates. For a warrior like Zadkiel that would be hell.

Zadkiel must have gleamed from Michael's face the train of his thoughts because he quickly added, "Sorry to disturb you. But I have news. There has been another attack."

Tory's gasp covered up Michael's violent curse. "Where?" he snapped.

"Chicago. But this witch has survived, and I thought you might want to question her."

Michael sensed the tension drain from Tory's limbs. This was good news indeed. But speaking with this witch would require he leave Tory alone. He couldn't teleport with her and a lot could happen in the amount of time it would take him to travel by human means. What if this was Asmodeus's plan, leaving the witch alive to draw him away from Tory?

"You must go," Tory said, as if sensing his hesitation. And it was very likely she could. They were bound, after all.

He reached up, gently palming her cheek. "Only if you promise to cast yourself inside the circle upstairs."

At her vigorous nod, Michael grasped the back of her neck, drawing her lips back to his, taking gentle command of her mouth. If there was one thing he could be thankful for, it was sharing his immortality. And since they were bound, if Asmodeus did make an appearance while he was gone he would know it almost instantly. Tory would be damn near impossible to kill now.

Pulling back, he gave her a gentle nudge toward the staircase, lightly swatting her ass when she frowned over her shoulder. Michael watched until she disappeared from view then turned to find Zadkiel studying him.

He arched a sardonic brow and Zadkiel grinned. "I see the deed has been done."

Michael growled. "Which deed? The one getting me eternal hellfire? Or the one that will draw torment and ridicule from everyone we know?"

If Zadkiel's grin had grown any bigger, Michael would have hit him. "One? Both? Take your pick."

"You're such an asshole," Michael muttered.

Zadkiel's only reply was laughter. *Make that two centuries of courier duty.*

Motioning with his hand, he invited Zadkiel to lead the way. Once the other male had teleported from the room, Michael closed his eyes, let his molecules divide until he was nothing but air and followed.

Chapter Seven

Tory paused at the top of the stairs, Michael's belligerent tone catching her attention. She wasn't eavesdropping, but she couldn't help that their voices carried up the stairs. Hellfire? Ridicule? What was he talking about? What deed had been done?

God, if they were discussing what she thought they were discussing she would be eternally mortified.

After waiting a few more seconds, she heard nothing else of interest, only silence. Tory contemplated sneaking back downstairs. That was when a weird sensation hit her, slamming into her chest and sucking the air from her lungs. In a panic, she tripped, bumping into the wall, her nails scraping at the surface as she tried to catch her balance.

The moment passed as quickly as it had occurred, leaving her breathless and disoriented. Stumbling down the stairs, her only intent to reach Michael, Tory found the living room empty, all trace of Michael gone.

Sweet Jesus, what had just happened?

Then she felt him, like a phantom caress in her chest, Michael surrounding her, stilling her fear. Faint whispers in her mind reassured her all was well, she was loved, protected. It was the strangest feeling sensing him in the deepest recesses of her psyche when he wasn't really there. But it also quenched the uncertainty and terror.

Tory took the stairs two at a time, the murmurs in her head egging her on, reminding her of her promise. By the time she reached the attic she was trembling from the rush of adrenaline.

Damn Michael. He had her in a mild state of panic when there was absolutely no need. Asmodeus had last been spotted in Chicago. He was still a long way from Boston. And anyway, there was no reason to assume he was any closer to finding her than he had been twenty-four hours ago.

After stepping into the middle of the pentagram, Tory went through the ritual of quickly reconnecting the white line she'd broken to release Michael. She recited the spell, enclosing herself within the safety of the circle.

As the minutes ticked by, Tory began to wish she'd brought a book, something, anything to pass the time. Food would have been good too, since she was getting hungry. And she had to pee.

A quick glance at her watch showed only fifteen minutes had gone by, damn it. She was never going to make it. If Michael didn't return soon, she was going to lose her freaking mind.

Another ten minutes and Tory couldn't wait any longer. It was her own fault for thinking about it. Now she couldn't concentrate on anything else. If she didn't go to the bathroom soon she was going to pee her pants.

And she was still hungry.

It would serve Michael right if she ended up dead. How long did it take to ask some chick a couple of questions? It wasn't exactly like he had to factor in travel time or anything.

Sucking in a deep breath, Tory knew she wasn't being fair. Recanting the spell, she reminded herself the poor woman had been attacked, could still be hanging on death's door right now and certainly deserved a little bit of Michael's time.

Though she would seriously prefer the witch find her own

angel.

That consideration stopped Tory in her tracks. The thoughts swirling around in her mind were really uncharacteristically nasty, especially the ones involving Michael anywhere near the witch in Chicago. She wasn't normally the jealous type, or at least she didn't think she was. Truthfully, she'd never had anything to be jealous about before Michael but still...

Tory shrugged as she descended the staircase, heading toward the bathroom. Maybe she was the jealous type. So shoot her.

After hitting the bathroom, Tory grabbed a spoon and bowl, a box of Captain Crunch and half a gallon of milk before heading slowly back up the stairs. She didn't want to get back into the circle but she knew if she wasn't there when Michael returned he would be plenty mad. He'd be sure to go all ballistic on her and Tory would find herself a virtual prisoner in her own home.

That would suck.

With her hands full, Tory tried juggling the door and her goodies before finally discovering she had to back her way into the attic to get through the doorway. When she swung back face forward, she found standing between her and the circle a man. Evil emanated from him in waves, totally contradicting his beautiful appearance. The need to vomit damn near brought her to her knees, and her box of Captain Crunch ended up on the floor, the first casualty of the evening.

Over six-and-a-half feet of ripped blond maleness rushing toward her might not have sent her into a panic, but the blood-curdling growl and the long steel blade aimed directly at her certainly did. Tory spun to the right, using the only weapons at her disposal, the half-gallon of milk and ceramic bowl to beat the intruder back. Hardly effective, neither did enough damage to help her get away. The milk bounced off his chest and he used his sword to bat the bowl away, sending it careening into the wall.

The only chance Tory saw of escaping the demon was the stairs, but she hated the thought of turning her back on him. As if she really had any chance of getting away. It was so unfair—just when she finally had something to live for.

She'd barely moved in that direction when she felt the first sting of his blade piercing her back. With a startled cry, Tory lunged forward, fire burning through her veins. She stumbled, her knees buckling, and she crashed to the floor, a sob ripping from her chest as the blade pierced her again, deeper this time. Gasping for breath, she tried to crawl away, but the floor under her was too slick and she collapsed in a heap on the wood.

"Die, bitch. Die," the inhuman voice snarled and Tory was pretty certain the bastard was going to get his wish. Death's icy grip was descending over her, and within its cold embrace the pain and fear began to slide away. As peace replaced horror, she finally embraced the darkness.

Chapter Eight

It turned out the witch lived in one of those chic condos in downtown Chicago overlooking Lake Michigan. Unlike Tory's home, where her nearest neighbor was miles from her, Evie Stanton's was only a wall away, and Michael couldn't fathom how no one had heard her screams.

As he approached the woman her eyes grew larger with each step. By the time he'd come to a halt right in front of her they were the size of saucers. At one time this would have pleased Michael greatly. He would have viewed it as a sign of respect. But that would have been LBT or Life Before Tory. Now it just annoyed the shit out of him.

"What did the demon want from you?" he demanded. His voice was a little harsh and Evie flinched. Michael knew he was frightening her, and he probably should have felt bad. But damn it, Evie Stanton was hardly on death's door. Hell, she'd only been kicked around a little bit. Michael figured there was a reason for that. Asmodeus had gotten what he'd come looking for.

"Michael, Ms. Stanton has been through a difficult time." Skath, the angel whose soul purpose was to govern the spell casters, approached. His tone was a gentle reprimand, and Michael watched Evie's gaze swivel to Skath, her look changing from one of a frightened rabbit to blatant hero worship.

He growled. "I am aware Ms. Stanton has been through a

difficult couple of hours, but even as we speak there is a demon hunting witches, and I'll be damned if I let him succeed in killing his target."

His snarl must have been more brutal than intended because it drew a whimper from Evie, and the woman leaned closer to Skath, who patted her back softly. "Just tell Michael what you can, dear, so he can be on his way. You want him to make the demon pay for his treatment of you, don't you, Evie?"

Evie nodded, tears welling in her eyes before slowly spilling over her lashes. "He had this little brown teddy bear and demanded I scry for the owner, a little girl, he claimed. But I kept seeing a woman, blonde hair, about five-three, and that angered him."

Michael tried to tell himself it could have been anyone Evie Stanton had seen. Five-three blonde-haired women were not uncommon, especially not with the invention of in-home dye kits. It didn't mean she had actually seen Tory.

"He kept insisting I was wrong. I was weak. Then he hit me. Kept hitting me..." Evie left off on a sob, burying her face in Skath's chest. Her slender shoulders shook and Skath grimaced over the top of her head.

Michael nodded for him to continue prodding her. The woman hadn't said anything telling him whether or not Asmodeus had discovered information concerning Tory, but Skath grimaced and swiftly shook his head. Michael could feel a headache beginning to form, an insistent pounding right behind his eyes. Jesus, he really hated dealing with humans.

"What else did you see?" he finally demanded because it was apparent Skath wasn't going to.

"Boston."

The one word mumbled into Skath's shirt sent a chill down Michael's spine and as a vicious curse was ripped from his chest, Evie began whimpering again. "Damn it, I'm not going to touch you. Did you tell the bastard anything else?"

When the woman didn't respond, only vigorously shook her head, Michael turned away, striding back to Zadkiel who stood waiting on the opposite side of the room.

"Well?" his second questioned.

"The woman revealed Tory's location. I must return to her immediately!" And as soon as Michael spoke her name, like a punch in the gut, he knew something was wrong. "Son of a bitch," he snarled, teleporting to his mate's location.

It took a minute for him to gain his bearings, for his body to adjust. In his confusion, he couldn't understand the form huddled on the floor inches from the staircase or the larger hulking figure standing over it, screeching and shielding its eyes. The presence disappeared before Michael could react, a small fraction of time he knew would haunt him for eternity, and then he realized what the motionless mass on the floor was.

"Tory!" Her name tore out of him like thunder.

Michael rushed to her side before falling to his knees. Gathering her into his arms, he cradled her broken and bleeding body to his chest. He felt the cry bubbling up from his chest, forcing its way from his lips, and he clutched his mate to him, rocking her gently as he buried his face in her neck.

It couldn't end like this. It wasn't fair. All these centuries he'd spent protecting humans and he couldn't keep one little woman from harm.

When the wetness hit Michael's face he did not immediately recognize it for what it was. Tears. His tears. For the first time in his long existence, he was weeping. Even Lucifer's betrayal had not brought him to his knees.

"My love, don't do this to me," he whispered, his voice hoarse, forcing him to choke out the words. "I won't be able to survive without you. I am not strong enough."

It's funny really, what one considers when they believe they have hit bottom.

How the hell had Gabriel endured?

It was in that moment Michael realized even in the midst of his heart-wrenching sorrow he could still feel her soul inside him. It had not fled this dimension. In fact, it had never left her body. She lived. And then he remembered the blood he'd shared with her.

He was a fool.

He willed a small dagger into his palm and used the pointed edge to puncture his fingertip. A few drops of blood oozed from the wound before Michael thrust his finger into Tory's mouth, rubbing it against the inside of her cheek. But he didn't dare allow her to consume too much. He only wanted to give her enough to aid in her healing, not to turn her, forcing her to exist on his blood.

Raining kisses along her hair, her face, her neck, Michael gave thanks that he'd already had the forethought to take the necessary steps in prolonging her life. And considering how close she'd come to death, Tory might not want to remove his balls with a dull, rusted knife when she gained consciousness.

Well...he could hope. Sometimes humans got testy about their mortality.

Gently lifting her into his arms, Michael cradled her against his chest before slowly rising, careful not to jostle her and cause her anymore pain. With extreme care, he descended the stairs and moved toward the bedroom, stopping only when his knees brushed the mattress.

The sheets were still rumpled from when they'd made love, reminding Michael of the sense of home he'd found within his mate's willing body. It only made him more determined to secure their future. Asmodeus would die for what he'd done to Tory and it no longer seemed to matter to Michael who delivered the killing blow. He would have all of his available warriors out scouring for the bastard because he intended to make certain the threat to his mate was eradicated. For good.

Except Zadkiel. Michael had a very special task for his second. Until Asmodeus was found he could not risk leaving Tory alone. But the portal to Heaven still needed to be located. As Zadkiel was the only other individual who understood the necessity in finding the damn thing quickly, he would leave no stone unturned until the job was done.

But before contacting Zadkiel with his new orders, Michael stripped Tory of her stained clothing, immensely relieved to find some of the wounds already closing. Gently cleansing her body, he removed all traces of blood from her skin. He would not have her waking still covered in the reminder of her attack. Then he hid her nudity underneath one of his T-shirts, an archaic sense of pride filling him in seeing his clothing draped across her skin.

Glancing down, he was reminded of the fact he was also covered in her blood. He couldn't have her rouse to find him in this condition. After taking a quick shower, he dressed before returning to her side. She was still unconscious—she didn't appear to have moved an inch—so after quickly examining her wounds once again and finding them continuing to heal, Michael drew the blankets over her before leaving her to rest.

But he didn't go far, only to the living room. From there he summoned Zadkiel, who immediately appeared. Michael wasted no time making his demands known.

"I want Asmodeus dead. Now. Have every available warrior hunting that bastard down. Pull those not involved in life-and-death situations and find him."

"Should he be held for you to dole out punishment?" Zadkiel questioned with a sardonic twist and Michael folded his arms across his chest.

"It doesn't matter who kills him as long as he does not escape again."

Surprise danced across Zadkiel's face. "What has happened?"

Michael shook his head. He really didn't want to give voice to the words. The knowledge of Tory's attack left a sick feeling in the pit of his stomach. "He was here," was all he could manage to force past his lips and it was enough. Zadkiel turned white as a sheet.

"Good God. Is she okay?"

With a brisk nod, he turned his back on his second and strode across the room to stand next to the couch and stare sightlessly out the window. "She will live. Asmodeus had best not."

"I'll get right on it."

"Zadkiel, wait," Michael called, twisting quickly to catch the other male before he disappeared. Zadkiel paused, his look questioning.

"I have a special assignment for you. I want you to hunt for the portal."

This must have surprised Zadkiel because his forehead furrowed, eyes narrowing, and he grew contemplative. "The portal? Well, I can't say I saw that one coming but I should have."

Michael glanced away, a niggling sense of guilt beginning to fester. "I will not allow Tory to be terrorized in such a way again."

"You do realize if you do this she will no longer be a secret. You will not be able to hide her in Heaven."

Returning his gaze to Zadkiel's, he nodded. "Any humiliation or punishment I would be forced to endure is nothing compared to her safety. Tory is my only concern. The rest is incidental."

With his head cocked to the side, Zadkiel studied him for a moment before responding, "I will do as ordered, my—"

"No," Michael hastily interrupted. "I am asking this as a special favor. For me."

A slow smile spread across Zadkiel's face. "You know, this is the first time you've ever asked for my help."

"And hopefully the last," he mumbled under his breath. "I'm sure you'll see you are suitably compensated."

"Let's just say you'll owe me," Zadkiel said with a chuckle. "You are not the first to find his mate and I'm sure you won't be the last. I might need that favor someday."

Michael snorted. God forbid Zadkiel mate. He needed someone he trusted to retain their faculties. This whole mating business drew a male to the edge of insanity. He'd been breaking one covenant after another since he'd first set eyes on Tory.

A weight lifted from Michael's shoulders as Zadkiel faded from sight. It was good to know someone had his back. Once upon a time, it would have been Gabriel riding shotgun.

With a sigh, he decided it was best not to think about Gabriel right now. Tory should awaken soon. Maybe later he could find a way to mend the cosmic gap between him and Gabriel, but for now Tory was his one and only priority.

Chapter Nine

Asmodeus paced the tiny confines of his chamber, hissing in frustration. The bitch still lived. Why? He should be free. Why was she not dead?

It wasn't from lack of trying on his part. He'd stabbed the bitch enough. But she'd continued to hang on. And then that sanctimonious bastard, Michael, had appeared. Michael. What the hell was he doing showing up? He never involved himself in the workings of humans. It was like a cardinal rule or something.

Ripping a hand through his hair, Asmodeus still couldn't get over the shock. The fucking archangel Michael. He was growing weak. That's why the son of a bitch had almost caught him. He'd known he would grow to regret letting the witch in Chicago live, but he'd been in such a hurry, thinking the end was within his grasp. Well, there was nothing else to do but find another meal. Something to last him several days. Then he would return and finish the job.

That drew a smile to his face. Yes, kill the bitch.

He came to a sudden halt, it finally hitting him. The look on Michael's face just before he'd fled. The anguish. The fear. It was what had struck him wrong. Michael cared about the woman. She was important to him.

Could it be that easy? Could he possibly kill two birds with one stone?

If he could defeat the mighty Michael... Oh, how Lucifer would reward him. He'd set Asmodeus up as his right-hand man. And without Michael around there would be no one to stop them. They'd take their rightful places on Earth. As gods. Corralling the humans like cattle, feasting on their souls until they were too full to move.

Then Lucifer would be next. If he could wipe out Michael, what was stopping him from going all the way and taking over Hell? He'd be *it*. King of Hell.

Yes. King was good. Very good.

Chapter Ten

Tory woke, panic rolling through her, chagrined when she was unable to recall the reason. She couldn't even remember how she'd ended up in bed. The clock on the nightstand read eight, which was obviously a.m. given the amount of sunlight flooding the bedroom.

Wait. How did it get to be daylight? The last thing Tory remembered was darkness had just fallen and Michael was leaving...but he was worried...about something. A demon?

Yes. That was it. A demon.

Tory jerked upright, the memory of the attack crashing over her. The demon's damn sword had pierced her flesh over and over again. She'd never in her life encountered anything so painful. Not even when, at the age of twelve, she'd seriously botched up a spell and set her pants on fire.

This time though, the culprit hadn't been a tiny little fire one of the stooges could put out with a great gust of wind. No, the sword had plunged into her, shredding major organs and destroying her from the inside out. She should be dead. At the very least, in the hospital clinging to life. So unless weeks had passed while she was out cold, something was very, *very* wrong.

Carefully edging off the bed, Tory expected pain but encountered only mild tenderness as she hobbled to the bathroom. Lifting the shirt that hung past her knees, she glanced down and spotted a thin white line where she was certain the blade had exited when it had gone through her body. A sense of panic overwhelmed her and, twisting in front of the mirror, she inspected her back, finding only a few areas of puckered skin. She tried to suck in a deep breath but a wheeze was all she accomplished as she fought back the terror.

What sounded like the door to the bedroom crashing into the wall drew tension through her until she heard Michael's bellow.

"Tory! Love, what is it?"

Storming from the bathroom, she slammed the door behind her before meeting him in the middle of the room. "What the hell happened to me?" When the only response to her demand was a guilt-stricken look, she added, "What did you do to me?"

Michael refused to answer, turning his back on her and moving toward the window in a blatant attempt at avoidance.

"Is it that terrible?" she whispered, a sense of dread filling her. While she couldn't imagine what it could be—she was alive after all—Michael's actions confirmed it was bad.

He sighed, and then softly said, "I gave you some of my essence."

Tory felt her forehead wrinkle in confusion. Essence? What the hell was he talking about? "You didn't use a condom during sex. Is that what you mean?"

Michael shook his head slowly. "There was no need the first time. Until we bonded pregnancy was impossible and we angels do not suffer from mortal disease. No, Tory, I fed you my blood."

"Eww. Your blood? What the hell did you do that for?" she demanded as she strode across the room, not stopping until she was standing right behind him.

Michael swiveled to face her, his piercing gaze meeting hers. "To make you immortal, my love."

Okay, Tory hadn't expected that to come from his mouth. "Immortal?" she repeated dumbly and Michael nodded. "Like immortal, immortal?"

His lips curved into a slight smile. "There's only one kind of immortal, love. You either are or you're not."

"But how?" Tory felt like she was repeating herself, but she couldn't grasp the concept.

"It was my blood, Tory. Too much and you turn into a vampire. Just enough and mortal death is no longer an option."

"But I can still die?" she asked, getting there was a distinction.

"Yes. There is a poison Lucifer managed to develop from corrupted souls, but even it is not certain death. And not something just any demon is able to get his hands on. Only Lucifer and his most trusted, of which Asmodeus is not."

Resting her head over his heart, Tory let the steady rhythm soothe her. Immortal she could deal with. Vampire she could not. She'd been raised to have an unrelenting fear of the creatures. Then again, they drank blood and there were all kinds of wrong about that.

"Okay."

Michael lifted her face, an arched brow meeting her gaze. "Okay? That's it? Just okay?"

"Yes. Okay." Pulling free from his grasp, she returned her head to his chest. "But no more blood. Vampires freak me out."

"I'm not surprised," he said, chuckling hollowly. "It was a vampire who killed Ariadne."

Tory jerked her head, bumping into Michael's chin. She winced, her hand drifting to rub the spot as she stepped away from him. "Lord, I don't even want to know. I have enough aches and pains without contemplating that one."

Michael wrapped an arm around her waist, gathering her to him as he guided her to the bed, clucking like a mother hen the whole way. "Why didn't you tell me you hurt? Rest now," he ordered, pulling the blankets back. But she sat on the edge of the bed, shaking her head.

"What about Asmodeus?"

"Don't worry about him," Michael stated, gently pushing at her shoulders, trying to get her to lie back and sleep. "You need your rest."

Knocking his hands away, Tory growled in frustration. "I will rest once I know what I should expect from the damn demon trying to kill me, Michael, and not a minute before."

He stilled, assessing her as if he were trying to determine her seriousness. With a sigh, Michael sank beside her on the bed. Clasping her hand tightly in his, he drew it into his lap, appearing to study their entwined fingers. Tory's patience began to wane quickly.

"I figure by now Asmodeus has realized you are not dead, which means he did not acquire whatever it is he is after. Now, if he is familiar at all with humans, he might expect you to linger a day or two. But after that he's going to realize something is not right. And that is when we can expect him to return to finish the job. Only this time he will be met with the surprise of his eternally damned life. Me. Unless my warriors find him first, of course. Then the threat will be neutralized."

"And we can get on with our lives." Tory smiled brightly, but the look in Michael's eyes had it sliding away.

"You do understand, Tory, he is only the first. You are going to be an amazingly powerful witch once you learn the extent of your true powers. Others will come unless..."

She waited for him to continue, but Michael seemed reluctant so she prodded, "Unless what?" When it didn't seem like he was going to answer, she added, "I swear, if this is our future, Michael, you hiding things from me, you can just keep it." Tory rose to her feet and tugged her arm in an attempt to gain her freedom. But Michael yanked back and, losing her balance, she ended up in his lap.

"I want you to return with me, to Heaven."

Now she stared at him flabbergasted. Was he serious? "How is that even possible?"

"There is a portal, but its location has been lost over time. I have Zadkiel searching for it as we speak. It is how you shall gain access."

"And if I decide not to?"

Michael rested his forehead against hers and sighed. "You really do not want me to answer that."

"So you are only pretending to give me a choice."

"You don't understand what it did to me, to find Asmodeus standing over your bloody form. I cannot go through that again."

Michael's response floored Tory. She was the one who had suffered the horror of being run through with a sword. Granted, she had probably blocked out a lot of the details and not everything was totally clear. And she was almost certain the recollection of pain had also dimmed. But still. He was making it all about him and it just pissed her off.

"What about me? I was the one stabbed. I don't really want to go through it again either."

"Then come with me," Michael bellowed.

"Fine," Tory yelled back.

For one stunned moment, Michael stared at her, his eyes wide. And then he laughed. "Love, you are going to be the death of me."

"As if," she mumbled in reply because his lips had already taken control of hers.

Winding her arms around Michael's neck, Tory arched into him, her breasts flattening against his chest. Who would have ever thought little Victoria Bloom, the misfit, the freak, could ever find such bliss? Her soul mate. She was still coming to terms with what it all meant.

She would never be alone again.

Her sob was captured by Michael's mouth as the overwhelming urge to worship every inch of him overtook her. Tearing her lips from his, she grasped the edge of his T-shirt. She was desperate to tug it up over his chest but her fingers kept getting tangled in the material. Chuckling, Michael knocked her ineffective hands away before pulling the shirt over his head. Once it was no longer in her way, Tory attacked, running her hands over taut muscles as her lips latched onto one tanned nipple. Michael groaned, his hand cupping the back of her head, fingers tangling in her hair.

"Do you like that?" she asked a little uncertainly.

"If I liked it any more I'd come in my jeans."

His response drew a smile to her lips. With one final lick, she pulled away, ignoring the slight tugging in her hair, and lifted her eyes to meet his. "I want you naked on the bed," she murmured.

Michael lifted a brow, echoing her grin. "Do you now?" he murmured.

"Yes, I do." She reached down to run a hand over his covered cock, already rock hard. "And I think you'll enjoy it."

Michael closed his eyes, a shudder rippling through him as she squeezed lightly, massaging his flesh with a teasing hand. His hips jerked. The low moan escaping his clenched teeth caused Tory to shiver.

"Shit," he hissed before grabbing her wrist in his tight grip. "Keep that up and it will be over far too quickly."

She leaned forward, her lips hovering over the shell of his ear. "Then strip. Now."

Michael's entire body jerked this time, then he jumped to his feet, shoving his jeans and underwear down in a frantic rush. He stood proudly in front of her, his cock only inches from her face. Tory circled her palm around the base, marveling at the feeling of silk over steel. Tightening her grip, she pumped from root to tip, smearing the drop of precome around the slit before tugging gently, forcing Michael closer.

She studied the organ, watching more wetness leak from the eye as she fondled the head and her curiosity grew, wondering how he would taste. Flicking her tongue out, she lapped at the meaty cap, dragging a groan from Michael's chest. His fingers returned to her hair, tangling through the strands, drawing her face closer to his body.

"Damn it, Tory. You're killing me. Open your mouth, love. Suck me in."

Complying with his breathless demand, she wrapped her lips around the head, running her tongue under the glans. Her hands grasped his thighs for balance, feeling the tension building with each pass of her tongue. She'd never thought she'd have this opportunity to give the man she loved pleasure, and now that she was here, that she actually could, she was rushing toward a high she'd never expected.

Michael began a gentle rocking motion, pushing his cock a little farther into her mouth with each pass. Tory wrapped a hand around the root to keep him from gagging her. Setting a rhythm, she pumped the base each time she sucked the head past her lips. Her teeth lightly scraped the shaft, dragging another groan from him.

"Play with my balls, Tory. Roll them in your hand."

His pleading tone had her palming his testicles, the soft furry sacks feeling so different from the hard shaft in her mouth. She experimented, squeezing them gently in her hand before milking them with her fingers.

"That's it, love," he whispered hoarsely. "You feel so damn good."

Lifting her eyes, Tory found Michael's torrid gaze on her, watching as his dick disappeared into her mouth. His face was pulled tight in a grimace, his teeth clenched as if he fought for control, and Tory loved every minute of it. She felt powerful.

His fingers tugged the strands of her hair. "Pull back, Tory, or I'm going to come," he demanded, which only incited her to suck harder. Michael groaned roughly. "I mean it, Tory. I can't hold on." It only took him a few seconds to realize she had no intention of stopping. His hands went from trying to gain his freedom to gripping the back of her head. "All right, love. You want it, here it comes." He surged forward, forcing the head of his cock to the back of her throat.

Tory gagged only a second before her throat opened, accepting the intrusion. His cock pulsed against her tongue, semen shooting from the tip. Michael cried out and there was nothing else she could do but swallow the creamy fluid. Tory kept her suctioning lips around him, drinking every last drop until he was spent. When she released him, Michael stumbled away from her.

Breathing heavily, he sagged to the mattress, his pants still hanging around his knees. The amusing sight had Tory chuckling and, as he pulled her into his arms, he said, "Give me a second and I'll return the favor."

"You already have," she whispered, laughter fading away. "You've given me more than I ever expected just by being here."

Michael rolled her under him, his hands brushing her hair back as he gazed into her eyes. "I could say the same, my love. I love you, Victoria Bloom."

Nodding, Tory was surprised to feel his cock growing hard against her abdomen. "I want you inside me now."

Michael groaned softly. "Then open up for me, love. Wrap your legs around my waist."

Tory did, giving a soft cry when she felt him entering her slowly. Her first climax took her by surprise, starting before he was even embedded completely within her. Michael cursed, fisting the bedding on both sides of her head as he retreated then thrust deep. Setting a steady rhythm, he prolonged her first orgasm, sending her falling headfirst into another almost immediately.

Her nails dug into his shoulders, her thighs tightening around him as she arched up, meeting each deep plunge. The third time she came the tremors ripped through her entire body, dragging breathy sobs from her throat, and above her Michael tensed, groaning into her ear.

Tory clung to him, never wanting to lose the security of his arms around her. While the prospect of leaving Earth to remain with him frightened her, she wouldn't let fear stop her from grabbing hold of happiness with both hands. She had been alone for too long to be foolish enough to let love slip from her grasp.

Chapter Eleven

Forty-eight tension filled hours later and still no demon. Asmodeus had left a trail of bodies all along the East Coast with no rhyme or reason. Michael's warriors had been chasing their own asses, unable to locate the bastard, and Michael was strung up tighter than a bow.

Tory was doing her best to entertain him, enticing him with sex, but even that had failed to relieve the stress. Not that Michael would dare complain—he wasn't a fool. But he feared getting too distracted would lead to disastrous consequences, namely Tory skewered on the end of a sword.

Michael slid under the spray of water, rinsing the soap suds from his body and wishing he had accepted Tory's offer to join him. Being as it was only about an hour until dawn, he'd declined, believing the likelihood of Asmodeus popping in this close to sunrise next to nil. But he didn't like having her out of his sight.

After turning off the water, he grabbed a towel from the rack and then wrapped it around his waist without really bothering to dry off. He could sense Tory's frustration. She'd been heading up the attic stairs determined to try casting some sort of locater spell when he'd walked into the bathroom. Finding Tory new spells to occupy her time was about the only thing those two stooges were good for.

Michael made a stop in the bedroom to dress before

beginning the climb up the narrow staircase. Halfway up a loud boom damn near shook the foundation and his first thought was of Asmodeus. He yelled Tory's name, taking the rest of the stairs two at a time, not slowing until he'd crossed the threshold.

The attic was filled with wisps of smoke and the smell, like burning hair, was nauseating. Michael buried his nose in the neck of his shirt, eyes watering as he scanned the room for Tory. And he found her all right, stomping out the last few sparks of what had apparently been another small fire. It was the third in two days. His mate would have made a splendid pyromaniac if it had been intentional.

She had the good grace to blush when she saw him standing there, arms folded across his chest.

"I don't understand why I can't get this," she said, her tone whining and causing Michael to clench his jaw. It wasn't the first time they'd started a discussion in such a way and he feared probably not the last. He wondered if he would be doing the universe a favor by finding someone to bind Tory's magic.

"Love, I don't understand why this is difficult for you. You are a very powerful witch."

"Me either," she whispered, approaching him. She took hold of his wrists, guiding them around her waist as she rested her cheek over his heart.

He held her tightly, hearing the tears she was trying to hold back in her voice. Burying his face in her hair, he breathed in the subtle scent of vanilla. It never failed to soothe him. The same way wrapping his arms around Tory seemed to do for her. She finally sighed and sagged against him.

"Do not fret. As soon as we have things settled here I will have Skath recommend another witch to help train you. It will be okay. I promise you, my love."

He felt her nod against his chest and relief wash through her. The strengthening of their mate-bond had been growing over the last forty-eight hours and already Michael could feel the varied emotions surging through Tory at any given time. Soon it would be even more than that. They would be able to communicate via a form of telepathy known as mate-speak, conveying all thoughts and feelings to each other in an incredibly intimate sharing of minds. Something he used to believe a huge deterrent toward mating but now couldn't wait to share.

A sudden disturbance in the air was Michael's first indication they were about to have company. A faint trace of sulfur was his second. Acting on instinct, he pushed Tory behind him as a faint pop reached his ears and Asmodeus appeared on the other side of the attic. He took immediate advantage of the demon's disorientation, charging his foe as he commanded his sword, Justice, to appear in his hand.

Justice, blazing a fiery yellow flame, was attracted to the evil emanating from Asmodeus. It was a weapon forged in Heaven for the single purpose of extinguishing the souls of the fallen, and it had been discovered any soul could be drawn into the fire. When the blade was hued red or orange those destined for the House of Souls could be trapped within the flame for later retrieval, but when the blade glowed yellow even those of pure intent could unwittingly be forever destroyed. Today Justice was eager for a demon's demise.

Michael swung at Asmodeus's torso, cursing when the demon met his advance. He'd hoped this would be easy. Not that Michael was fearful of losing to Asmodeus. The demon had, after all, been routed from Heaven by one of Michael's weaker warriors. Any other time Michael would have played with his quarry for the sheer fun of it. But Tory was in the room and he would not risk her getting caught in the crossfire.

"Tory, get in the circle now!" he called over his shoulder, barely sparing a glance in her direction. He didn't have to—he was very aware of her every movement as if her limbs were an extension of his own. And for once, she didn't argue with him.

Their clash had sent Asmodeus stumbling back a foot, but he regained his balance before Michael could destroy him. The pair circled each other. Michael, confident in his superiority, paid little heed to Asmodeus's gloating facade.

"Nothing will protect your little witch from me," Asmodeus taunted, his lips upturned in a smug smile. "Once you have been defeated, I will strip the flesh from her body inch by tiny inch. I might even let you watch while the life drains from you."

Michael rolled his eyes. Why did demons always feel the need to gloat before he killed them? "And you expect to do this how?"

"Don't you smell it, oh mighty Michael, the poison that will end your life?"

He felt Tory's gasp wash over him but refused to acknowledge her fear. He wouldn't give Asmodeus the satisfaction of seeing the demon's words had affected him. And it really didn't change anything. It couldn't. Not when Tory's wellbeing hung in the balance. Michael would have to be more careful, make certain Asmodeus's poisoned blade did not touch him.

"Bring it on." Completely blocking Tory from his mind, Michael egged the demon on, hoping in Asmodeus's delusions of grandeur he would attack first.

With a shriek that shook the rafters, Asmodeus lunged at him, granting Michael's wish. The demon's eyes were lit with eager anticipation. His sword arm already swinging, Asmodeus aimed for his gut. Michael reacted quickly, Justice spitting and popping as the two swords clashed. Pivoting and using the heel of his boot, Michael slammed his foot down on to the demon's toes, the howl of pain bringing him an ounce of satisfaction. He wanted Asmodeus to suffer tenfold for all the pain he'd caused Tory. Willing a dagger into his other hand, Michael slashed at the demon's side, feeling the steel slide through skin.

Asmodeus jerked away, spinning to face Michael. The smugness was now gone from the demon's features, his gaze warier. It should have made Michael ecstatic, but it didn't. He couldn't stop seeing Tory, lying bloody on the floor from the last attack. Shaking his head, he tried to clear his mind of the distraction, lurching backwards in time to avoid getting impaled by Asmodeus's poisoned blade.

With a gleeful cackle, Asmodeus followed. Michael knew if he didn't end the confrontation soon, eventually the demon would get lucky. While it wasn't the wound that would prove fatal, the poison would eat away at his soul slowly—the process long and agonizing until nothing remained of him but ash. Feigning to the right, the demon following, Michael then sprang to the left, getting behind Asmodeus before the demon had realized his mistake. Justice firm in his grip, he embedded the tip in Asmodeus's back.

The demon tried to jerk away, to rip free of his fate, but it was already too late. Justice glowed brightly. Great waves of yellow light surged into Asmodeus's torso, sizzling and snapping in a happy chorus. Sensing Tory's spike of fear, Michael wished he could move to comfort her. Instead, he braced his legs wide as pulsing waves of energy vibrated up his arm. The light grew larger, surrounding the demon entirely before flooding the attic with its intense glow. Everything, even the very air in the room, stilled for a brief moment and then all light and energy was sucked back into Justice with a resounding *pop*, leaving only a thin cloud of dust where Asmodeus had once stood.

Standing there, Justice still dancing in joyous waves, Michael barely recognized Tory had broken the seal on the circle of protection. He was too busy trying to get the wayward sword, which still sensed another soul in the room, under control. Holding her off with an outstretched hand, he yelled, "Stay back!" He then concentrated with all his might on Justice. "Evanesco," he commanded, and the sword disappeared.

Lowering his arm, Michael barely had time to prepare before Tory was jumping at him. "What the hell was that?" she demanded as he caught her, relishing the way she wrapped her limbs around him. Burying his face in her hair, he shook his head. He couldn't speak past the lump in his throat because for a minute there he hadn't thought Justice would heed his order.

"I love you, Tory" he whispered, his gaze drawn to the spot Asmodeus had stood. The threat was terminated. At least for now. But Michael knew it wasn't over. There would always be some demon attracted by her power, who thought he could make a name for himself. Until Zadkiel found the portal Tory would never be truly free. Thankfully, Zadkiel believed he was close. With his hand cupping her cheek, he drew Tory's head up, and his lips captured hers in a soft kiss.

"I love you too, Michael, my own personal avenging angel."

He chuckled quietly. He guessed he was because for this one little human, Michael would storm the walls of Hell itself. His to protect and cherish. Her avenging angel.

Epilogue

As Michael hid, immersed in the shadows, he recalled all he'd learned of his target. Like his Tory, she was small in stature. But what she lacked in height, she more than made up for in courage. And she was strong. She would have to be for what he intended.

He'd been a fool.

Sure, he'd given Gabriel's grief proper lip service. It had been a tragedy, a terrible circumstance of fate. But until he'd held Tory's broken and bleeding body in his arms, believing he would lose her, Michael had never truly understood all Gabriel had suffered.

Now was the time to correct the injustice that had occurred to one of his best friends. Creeping forward, he whispered, "Gladuis," and Justice appeared, its red flame breaking through the darkness. While the woman slept on, unaware of his presence, he placed the tip on her abdomen, displacing the soul he had captured into her womb where it immediately merged with the newly formed bundle of cells.

But Michael did not get away unseen. He hadn't counted on the man sensing his presence and was a bit disconcerted when the man emerged from a connecting room, his gun already drawn. A warrior in every sense of the word, he stopped wide-eyed as his gaze rested on Michael and Justice. A demon hunter. Michael couldn't help grinning. Gabriel would probably try to take off his head if he ever discovered Michael had once again marked Ariadne as a hunter. He figured it would probably be best not to mention it.

"I have given you a great gift," Michael said, glancing back at the still-silent woman before returning his gaze to her husband. "Protect them well, human. Both of them." Then Michael flashed from the room.

Returning to Heaven, Michael breathed a sigh of relief—mission accomplished—and headed back to the rooms he and Tory shared on the top floor of the Powers' headquarters. Zadkiel had been successful in finding the portal about one month after Asmodeus had been terminated, and Michael had smuggled her in the dead of night. Most still didn't know of her existence, only his warriors whom he trusted to keep their silence. He hoped to keep it that way for as long as possible. Not forever. Only twenty-five or so years until either Gabriel saw fit to forgive him or he was far too busy dealing with his own mate to give Michael problems.

After entering the headquarters, Michael hurried past Zadkiel, ignoring the fact he had begun speaking. If there was a problem Zadkiel would have to deal with it on his own. Michael didn't have time. Tory was waiting for him and she had a new spell she wanted to try, something involving levitation. Since she insisted they be making love when she spoke the magic words, Michael wasn't about to be delayed. And he figured getting a little singed would be worth it. Besides, she was getting better. The last time he'd only lost his eyebrows and they'd grown back.

About the Author

To learn more about Madelyn Ford, please visit www.madelynford.com Send an email to Madelyn Ford at madelynjford@gmail.com or join her Yahoo! group to join in the fun with other readers as well as Madelyn Ford. http://groups.yahoo.com/group/madelynford/

LaVergne, TN USA
23 March 2011
221260LV00006B/2/P